As his attacker landed on his back, his right arm was held at the wrist over the pivot of Jubal's forearm. The limb broke with a clear, sharp *click*, the jagged ends of bone spiking up through the soft flesh of his underarm.

He screamed, high and shrill like a wounded pig, until Jubal's boot smashed against the side of his neck.

Jubal whirled, conscious of someone moving up behind him. As he turned, he saw a circle of grey-clad men watching grimly, one of them coming forwards with a .36 Spiller and Burr revolver. . . .

Along a desolate trail in New Mexico, Jubal Cade stumbles upon a mysterious scene of slaughter. His promise to a dying man puts him on the trail of a mad albino general and plunges him into a demented world where ghostly armies fight a lost cause and DEATH WEARS GREY.

Jubal Cade / 8

# Death Wears Grey

Charles R. Pike

CHELSEA HOUSE
New York, London
1980

Copyright © 1980 by Chelsea House Publishers, a division of
Chelsea House Educational Communications, Inc.
First published in Great Britain in 1976 by Granada Publishing Limited
Printed and bound in the United States of America
LC: 80-69221
ISBN: 0-87754-237-6


Chelsea House Publishers
Harold Steinberg, Chairman & Publisher
Andrew E. Norman, President
Susan Lusk, Vice President

A Division of Chelsea House Educational Communications, Inc.
70 West 40 Street, New York 10018

# CHAPTER ONE

The column of smoke drifted lazily across the afternoon sky, shading from funereal black into grey as it drew a stark exclamation mark against the cloudless blue. Jubal Cade watched with cautious interest from the shadow of a side-slanting boulder; he knew that smoke rising through the baking air of a New Mexican noonday meant trouble, and that was a commodity he had dealt in too much of late. He slitted his deep-set brown eyes against the sun's glare and shifted his head slowly from side to side: peering straight at something through the heat haze told a watcher nothing. The slow sideways movement brought the whole panorama into vision, revealing the peripheral details that could tell a whole lot more of the story. Details like the fluttering black shapes that blended with the smoke as they spiralled lazily down towards the ground from their airborne vantage points: vultures looking for meat.

He sighed as he rose to his feet, pushing the grey derby down on his forehead to shade his eyes. He was a small man, no more than five feet six, and built slim, his build belying the wiry strength hidden beneath a soiled white shirt and grey pants; the matching jacket and vest that formed the remainder of his English-tailored suit were lashed across the saddle of the black horse whickering nervously beside him.

As he stood up, he settled the heavy Cavalry Colt hanging in a shoulder-rig on his left side to a more comfortable position and then walked over to the animal. He stroked its head, his hand moving unconsciously towards the butt of the Spencer rifle draped along the right-hand side of the saddle. The Spencer was a ·30 calibre Civil War model, a repeater converted from carbine to rifle by a man Jubal had once known, long ago and long dead in the holocaust that had threatened to rip America apart. Like the long gun, the Colt had also been

5

converted, to take the same ·30 shells. Jubal Cade was deadly proficient with either weapon.

He climbed into the saddle, settling himself with the habit of a man used to long hours on horseback, and walked the big black in the direction of the smoke.

Hell, he mused, smoke means trouble and that means hurt people. And I am a doctor.

For a painful moment, his mind travelled back to a past better forgotten, when he had been a medical student in England, a young man with ideals, burning to bring his healing skills to the frontiers of the West. He had brought them all right, he thought, along with his bride. And then seen Mary and his hopes die together.* Since then he had ranged the vastness of America searching for her killer, forgetting his ideals in the long vengeance hunt. Every once in a while, however, he was forced to remember.

And the scene that spread itself out before him as he pushed through the cacti proved to be one of those times.

Ahead of him the arid plain fell away in a shallow bowl about a quarter of a mile across. Around the indentation the cactus plants provided an encircling ring of camouflaging growth, broken only by the trail that came and went from east to west. Spread along the trail was a litter of wagons, dead horses, cattle and men. The smoke Jubal had spotted was billowing from a long-framed Conestoga towards the centre of the train; and the corpses were thickest there.

So were the vultures that heaved themselves skywards as he approached.

There was no overt sign of the attackers, and Jubal felt confident that the birds would not have come down if anything lived in the depression, but he still lifted the Spencer from its sheath and levered a shell into the breech as he rode down.

There was something wrong about the wagon train that he couldn't quite figure out. The seven wagons suggested a normal pioneer party, but that would have had women with it; wives, sisters, children. There were no women, nor any children, amongst the bodies, only men. And they looked – what

* See Jubal Cade – *The Killing Trail.*

6

was left to be seen, anyway – more like cowboys or gunhands than pilgrims on the road west. The dead cattle too seemed incongruous. Most wagon trains took a few milch cows along, either to use on the journey or for breeding purposes at journey's end, but the steers Jubal saw were the long-horned range cattle he had known in Texas. Maybe it was a trail drive, the tracks heading away from the massacre suggested a large number of cattle had been driven off; but a trail drive used only two or three wagons, not seven and not the kind standing lonely and lifeless before Jubal.

The whole thing was odd and he pulled back the hammer of his rifle in anticipation of trouble as he pushed towards the biggest wagon.

The voice lifted the small hairs along his spine and sent him powering sideways out of the saddle in a curling dive that left him belly-down in the sand with the Spencer angling towards the source of the sound. It seemed to come from inside the big Conestoga standing directly behind the burning wagon and Jubal rolled behind the shelter of a dead horse as he tried to spot the speaker.

The words were indistinct, a pain-filled moaning, but the crack of a pistol was definite enough. It sent Jubal's horse skittering away to the edge of the carnage and gave him the chance to pinpoint the lone defender.

'Ease up,' he yelled, staying behind the shelter of the horse, 'I'm friendly.'

'Like hell.' The words were clear and the shot that punctuated the brief sentence clearer still. It lifted tufts of hair from the horse's back and pushed Jubal's head down below the line of fire. Whoever had survived the attack was still dangerous, no matter how badly hurt he might be.

'I'm a doctor,' Jubal shouted. 'I figured you could use help.'

The answer was another bullet.

As it hit, Jubal lifted to his feet and darted in closer to the wagon, throwing himself down behind a heavy wood chest that lay on its side with the top swung open where it had been rifled. The glint of sunlight on the clasp caught his attention

7

and as a fourth bullet blew splinters high in the air, he noticed the insignia stamped into the metal. The embossing was rubbed and battered, but he could make out an etched illustration of crossed cannon barrels beneath faint lettering that said something about Stuart's Horse Artillery. The words rang faint bells of remembrance in Jubal's mind, but he was unable to say why. And stopped wondering as a fifth bullet ricochetted off the chest.

He hoped the man carried his pistol on an empty chamber as he powered headlong at the wagon, crossing the bloody sand in long paces straight at the Conestoga.

He came up hard against the side as a bloodied hand clutching a long-barrelled Navy Colt stuck through the canvas flap. The hammer fell on an unloaded breech as Jubal cracked the muzzle of his rifle hard across the wrist. The fingers holding the pistol straightened involuntarily so that it spun on the extended index finger before Jubal knocked it to the ground. Before it reached the sand, he was swinging over the side of the wagon, angling up and in to crash down on top of the hidden gunman.

Air exploded from the man's lungs in a frothy red spray as Jubal came down on his chest. He screamed once and then passed out, so that Jubal was left alone in the silence, broken now only by the hungry buzzing of the flies.

The man stretched out on the plank floor of the Conestoga was in his mid-forties, a big, dark-haired man with a heavy growth of beard stubble absorbing large quantities of the blood that ran from several scalp wounds. More serious were the patches of crimson speckling his grey jacket and blending with the red patches on his upright collar and cuffs. His outfit looked strangely like a uniform of some kind, but so faded now, and stained with blood, that Jubal had no idea what it might represent. He ignored it as he carried out a swift examination of the man's wounds. A cursory glance told him they were serious, a closer look emphasized his diagnosis: the man was dying from two bullet holes in his chest, one piercing his left lung, the other through his collar-bone. The three arrows sticking out of his back did nothing to help his condition and only an amazingly powerful force of will could have kept him alive this long.

Jubal shrugged and decided against using any of his carefully-hoarded supply of medicine on a lost cause.

Instead, he made the dying man as comfortable as possible and settled down to wait for him either to finish his lonely flirtation with oblivion or wake up. To Jubal's surprise, he woke up, pain-misted eyes glaring as he spotted the silent, waiting figure. His hand moved to his side, where a brown leather holster lay empty on his right hip. Jubal noticed it was reversed so the gun's butt would protrude forwards, Cavalry style, and smiled as the man cursed when he found it empty.

'Get it done, boy.' The words came thick through parched lips. 'Tyree ain't about to beg you for nothin'.'

'I'm not planning on killing you,' murmured Jubal. 'Like I said, I wanted to help.'

Tyree grinned, his face looking like a death-mask.

'Kinda late for that, but thanks anyways.' His voice, through the croak of pain, carried the soft drawl of the South. 'An' sorry I laid for you. Reckoned you was a 'Pache come back fer more hair.'

Jubal grinned and gestured at the grey jacket he had pulled on as the afternoon faded into early evening.

'Do I look like an Apache?'

Tyree twisted around to stare at Jubal, watching him with sudden interest that seemed to be focused not on Jubal's face, but on his clothes.

'Guess not,' he muttered, 'now that I got a close look at you.'

Painfully, he reached inside his blouse and withdrew two packages. Both were stained with the blood oozing from his chest and one was torn at the corner, where a slug had nicked it before ploughing through flesh. He held one out to Jubal, a flat square of sealed oilskin that carried heavy daubs of wax along the folds.

'Get that to Canfield. He's in Albuquerque now, waiting fer us.' He coughed more blood. 'Tell him what happened here. Ole Beauregard ain't gonna get his cattle or his guns.'

9

He broke off in a spasm of coughing that doubled him over the second packet, speckling the shiny oilskin with bright-red blood. Jubal looked at it, knowing from the colour that Tyree was fading fast.

'Look, friend,' he said softly, 'I'm heading for St. Louis, not Albuquerque. I'll post that on for you, but Albuquerque's a good hundred miles north of here.'

He stopped as Tyree's hand grasped his wrist, wrapping firmly over the cloth of his suit.

'Dammit.' The words came harder now, but the intensity was still there. 'You wear the grey, don't you? You gotta take it.' He dragged himself upright on the wagon bed. 'That's an order, mister! You got a duty: get that message to Canfield. Foul up an' I swear to God I'll come back from the fuckin' grave to get you.'

Jubal nodded slowly, easing Tyree's hand from his wrist. 'All right, I'll take it. Where do I find Canfield?'

'How the hell should I know? Ask around. You know as well as me that Canfield don't put up signs to his whereabouts.' Tyree coughed some more and pushed the other packet at Jubal. 'Take this too. Expenses fer the trip. Ain't none of us gonna use 'em.'

Jubal accepted the heavier package as Tyree spat the last remnants of his life over his trousers and died. Gently, Jubal lowered the body to the bed of the wagon, then, thoughtfully, opened the second envelope. It was a good eight inches long by four wide, and the contents bulked it out, hard and heavy. As the wax on the seals broke the solid glint of gold coins shone through, spilling into Jubal's palm. He set the envelope down and studied the coins. They were gold eagles and from the weight there had to be at least five hundred dollars' worth.

Jubal grinned as he hefted the coins, then he picked up the Spencer and climbed down from the wagon. Maybe he would find the mysterious Canfield in Albuquerque. It looked like he owed Tyree something, now.

As he walked over to his nervous horse he wondered about the dying man's words. It seemed as though Tyree had been a military man delivering some kind of confidential message; he

10

studied the sealed envelope and thought about opening it. Then he decided against his curiosity: the thing had to be more valuable if it was delivered intact. He pushed it into his saddlebag as he eyed the ravaged wagon train. From Tyree's dying words and the state of the corpses, it was obvious that Indians had attacked the travellers, run off their cattle and looted the wagons. But the basic set-up remained unexplained: too many wagons for a trail drive, too few women for a pioneer trek.

Jubal hitched the black to a wagon wheel and began to walk amongst the bodies.

The hair was mostly gone and the mutilations inflicted by the Apaches were attracting hordes of flies, but even beneath the obscuring detritus of death, the corpses bore a uniform similarity. Grey was the prevailing colour of their clothing; grey blouse-style jackets, like Tyree's; grey trousers, occasionally striped with red or faded yellow or pale blue. Too, many holsters were cross-hung in the reverse-grip fashion of the military. And there were several battered kepis scattered bloodily near the newly-bald heads of their owners, the kind troopers wore.

He wondered just what it had been that Tyree had died to bring to – what was his name? – Beauregard. Cattle, sure; Tyree had said that. And guns. But where was Beauregard, that a shipment of cattle and guns had to cross a section of territory no herder or trader in his right mind would attempt to cross?

Unless he didn't want to be seen. Unless he preferred to risk Apache attacks against some greater risk. Like being spotted by the authorities.

Jubal shrugged as he mounted the black horse. So maybe Tyree had been mixed up in something illegal, the man was dead now and he had paid Jubal to deliver a message; so that was what he would do – for five hundred dollars – and ask no questions. With the money in his pocket added to the gold he had picked up in San Rafael* he could afford to detour north to Albuquerque and pick up the train east from there. A few

* See Jubal Cade – *The Golden Dead*.

11

weeks of comfortable travel would see him, well-fed and rested, in St. Louis. That thought more than compensated for any doubts he might have briefly entertained about Tyree's operation.

There were too many corpses spread around to consider burying, so he kicked the black into an easy canter along the trail northwards, appreciating the solid chink of gold flapping heavily in the saddlebags.

He rode for two days without seeing anyone; long days of New Mexican sun that baked the dirt of the trail to a hard-packed dry red dust, and cold nights that crusted his blanket with frost crystals. He took it easy, not wishing to exhaust the horse in the unpopulated wilderness they were crossing. Then, on the third morning, he encountered a Cavalry patrol.

The column of blue-clad men rode out of the heat haze like mounted ghosts, shrouded in a mist of drifting dust that covered their uniforms in the same pale colour that obscured their horses. Jubal reined in at the side of the trail, waiting for them to come up alongside.

As the head of the column reached him, one grey ghost raised an arm and bellowed an order back down the file. It stopped with military precision as the lieutenant in command came up level with Jubal.

He slapped dust from his stetson as he studied the small, dusty man watching silently from the side of the trail. Then he saluted, grinning through the grime on his face.

'Lieutenant Docherty, U.S. Cavalry,' he announced. 'Maybe you can help us.'

'Hope so,' said Jubal easily, 'but how?'

'We're hunting renegades,' grunted Docherty, 'mess of die-hard Rebs running guns north. Have to confess I don't rightly know why a Reb would want to carry guns anyplace north of Joplin, but orders are orders.' He puffed heavily, as though he not only failed to understand the orders, but also doubted their sense. 'Anyways, we got news there was a column of wagons an' stuff moving this way, so the good old die-hard Seventeenth got its orders.' He shifted in his saddle. 'They don't call us the Sore-backs for nothing. Every damn' half-cock rumour that

12

comes out of Texas, Arkansas and points east gets followed up by us.'

He paused, smiling apologetically at his outburst, and offered Jubal his canteen. Gratefully, Jubal sipped on the brackish water, waiting for the question he had guessed would follow.

'Thing is,' said Docherty, 'we been tailing tracks out of a one-horse town called Consequences for three days now. You seen anything along the way?'

'Yeah.' Jubal gestured back over his shoulder. 'There's a bunch of wagons and men burned out back there. Could be the one you're looking for. If they left a town called Consequences, they sure paid for it.'

# CHAPTER TWO

The blue-coats moved out at a smart canter, eager to locate their elusive quarry and bring an uncomfortable mission to a swift conclusion. Jubal watched them go by in a swirling cloud of dust that drifted slow and lazy across the afternoon, obscuring their passage behind a sun-shafted curtain of grey as though they had faded away into the heat haze. He reached back, absently, to pat the saddlebag where the two oilskin packages rested. So it looked like Tyree had been a gun-runner, presumably carrying the weapons to the mysterious Beauregard with Canfield acting either as guide or middleman.

It made little difference to Jubal's plans. Whatever the moral implications of the ex-Confederates' venture might be, he had agreed to deliver a message. He had his reward, sitting reassuringly in his saddlebag, and he intended to carry out his promise to the dead man.

He pulled his sweat-soaked shirt clear of his chest, hoping for a cooling breeze that didn't come, and kicked the black into a trot in the direction of Albuquerque.

At noon he reined in, looking for shade. The black was drenched and blowing hard despite the easy pace Jubal had set, and its rider too was feeling the effects of the New Mexican sun. His clothes were sticky rags that clung with a gluey consistency to his body, rivulets of trickling, salty sweat ran down his face, misting his vision so that the stark shapes of the giant cactus plants danced behind a watery haze.

Gratefully, he spotted a clump of mesquite scrub standing high enough to afford shade and headed the horse towards that shelter. He dismounted and hauled the saddle off the animal's back before looking to his own comfort: he had no wish to see the beast develop saddle sores before he reached civilization. He tethered the black and poured water from his drying canteen into the cup of his own grey derby. When the horse had finished drinking, Jubal set the hat back on his head, luxuriating in the coolness imparted by the water, and took a drink himself. Then he squatted down and began to rummage through his saddlebags. He located the jerky stashed there and, his back comfortably settled against the trunk of a stunted tree, chewed on the dried meat.

It was by no means the most satisfying meal he had eaten, but he was hungry, his last meal having been breakfast, taken at sunrise when the desert was cooler and easier to cross, so he bit avidly into the solid wad of meat, washing it down with carefully-measured sips from his canteen. By the time he had finished, the sun was at its full zenith, burning out of the cloud-free sky like an angry white eye that bleached the land beneath its glare to its own bone-white starkness.

Mesquite and cacti shimmered and shifted in the glittering light, their contours hazed by the glare. The only shadows now, languid beneath the sun, were the dark pools around the bases of the plants and the wider area beneath the mesquite.

The land was totally quiet. No animals moved in the noon-day heat, no birds beat the burning air with their wings. Jubal was isolated in a tiny enclave of shadow, hot and silent in the burning wastelands. He stretched lazily, pulled a cheroot from his jacket and lit up, leaning back against the tree as he enjoyed the pungent black cigar. He smoked slowly, enjoying the luxury of the brief stop and the taste of tobacco in his mouth. When he had finished, he stubbed the cheroot into the sand and let his eyes close slowly. He had not meant to fall asleep, but the heat and the food combined to swathe him in a torpor that stuck his eyelids together and carried him gently off into a light doze.

He woke up with a start and the big, black bore of a ·50 calibre Sharps buffalo gun centred deadly steady between his eyes.

Instinctively, his hand reached towards the Spencer resting beside him; then conscious reflex brought the movement to an abrupt stop as the impossibility of the action registered on his mind. Down the long barrel of the huge gun he could see a gnarled and dirty thumb resting on the cocked hammer. A long time back he had fought men with guns like this and seen the devastating power of the mile-firing weapon.* At such close range he knew the slightest pressure on the trigger would lift his head in bloody tatters from his shoulders, so he relaxed, moving his head back as far away from the muzzle as he could.

Shifted back, Jubal was able to focus his eyes on the man holding the buffalo gun. And nearly moved again in sheer surprise.

Grinning at him over the sights of the rifle was a wrinkled, bearded face that might have been any age from sixty to something else. It was totally impossible to guess the man's age, so lined and weather-beaten was he. Pale blue eyes, set deep beneath taut-drawn lids, peered brightly with an insane glint from a mask of skin tanned dark enough to belong to a Negro. A curling moustache fell in silver-grey waves down into a chest-length beard of the same colour. The tan of the face was broken by deep lines that looked as though they might have been cut there by a knife blade; long lines crossed the forehead, curving lines hooked down from nostrils to mouth, behind the beard and moustache the man's lips were two thin, dried-out flakes of hard skin. Where he sweated in the heat, salt had crusted on the wrinkles, so that every deep-etched line was marked out whitely against the tan.

Strangely, no hair showed beneath the wide-brimmed Mexican sombrero set on the oldster's head. The hat itself was impressive enough, a tall-crowned affair that had once been, perhaps, black. Now, though, it was near-white with old sweat stains, its most definite colour coming from the band of gleaming silver dollars decorating the rim. Highly-polished, they glistened in the sun, which the strange figure seemed to ignore as it beat down upon his back. Rather, he pitched his head forwards, so that the reflected dazzle of the sun off the dollars threw blinding shafts of light into Jubal's eyes, dazing and confusing him as the man moved his head in little darting movements from side to side, back and forwards.

He was still grinning, showing black-stubbed teeth between

* See Jubal Cade – *Vengeance Hunt.*

16

the gummy gaps in his mouth, obviously enjoying the effect his bizarre appearance had on Jubal.

Unnervingly aware of the gun still pointed at his head, Jubal studied the rest of the stranger's appearance.

His shirt was a bleached buckskin thing, as old and wrinkled as his face, although worn long enough to fade the colour down several shades lighter than his skin. Hung around his waist was a black leather belt decorated, like his hat, with silver dollars; on his left hip, it carried a sheath with the bone handle of a long-bladed skinning knife protruding like a bad tooth; on the right a ·44 Remington Star was holstered in a softer leather scabbard that looked to be greased for fast work, and much used.

His trousers were a pair of faded levis, the leg stretched out nearest to Jubal displaying a dirty black boot that looked as though it had been cleaned round about the last time the man shaved.

The other leg ended just below the knee. It was stitched up tight with heavy thread that gathered the rough denim around the slender column of hickory wood sticking out where flesh and bone should have been.

Jubal couldn't help gasping in surprise as he realized that the weird figure was further misshapen by a wooden leg.

He took a deep breath and decided to take the initiative.

'Call me Jubal.' He broke off at the cackle that erupted as he spoke.

'Don't care too much what I call you.' The voice was dry as the scar on a cowboy's cheek and its sepulchral tones prompted Jubal to shudder like a snake in an eagle's beak. 'It ain't important. Not to me, anyways. Might be to you, though. To you it might just be the difference.'

The old man giggled, losing the sentence in a splutter of spittle.

'Difference?' Jubal was all too aware of the steady hands holding the buffalo gun, calm for all the cackling. 'What difference?'

'Difference 'tween livin' and dyin' is all,' coughed the strange figure, 'depending on the answers you give me.'

17

Jubal waited, conscious that the sun had shifted across the sky and that the mesquite patch had grown suddenly cooler.

The oldster sat, utterly still, as though time meant nothing to him, as though he would sit, crouched over the wooden stump of his right leg until Jubal answered whatever were his questions of his own accord.

'I can't answer questions I've not been asked.' Jubal was wondering if he might risk a grab for one of his guns anyway; the alternative seemed to be starving to death.

'Yeh. Guess that's true.' A gobbet of spittle accompanied the comment. 'Allus did like a man as came straight to the point.'

Bright eyes stared hard at Jubal, studying his face, his clothes, seeming to probe into his skull.

'First one is where'd you come from?'

'San Rafael.' There wasn't another town in miles and Jubal hoped the man was not a bounty hunter hired by the townsfolk to track him down. It seemed unlikely: he had left too much confusion behind him and there couldn't be too many bounty-men willing to take on so small a pursuit.

'San Raf', heh?' The interest was hedged. 'Been anywheres near Consequences?'

'Never had the pleasure.' Jubal didn't understand the way the conversation was taking, but he hoped to prolong it.

'Ever met folks from there?'

'Not that I know of,' said Jubal steadily, remembering Tyree and Lieutenant Docherty; 'why?'

The barrel of the Sharps darted out to clip his forehead.

'I'm askin' the questions, mister. You just sit tight an' answer. You got a whole lot hangin' on it.'

Jubal sat tight.

'You come up the road outta San Rafael. Looks to be like you're headin' fer Albuquerque an' there ain't but one way through along that trail. So; you see any folks on the way?'

'Some.' Jubal wondered who it was interested the old man so much.

'Like who?' There was immediate interest showing. 'Talk about them. That way you might get to live a while longer.'

18

Jubal decided on a long explanation.

'Like two groups. First one I found three days ago, all of them dead.' He saw no point in mentioning Tyree or the packages he was carrying. 'Wagon train, by the look of it. The Apaches hit them and wiped out the whole train. Ran off the cattle and just left corpses behind.'

He broke off again as the Sharps moved closer.

'What kinda corpses?'

'How many kinds are there?' Jubal countered, wondering how much this strange man knew.

'Don't piss me around.' The cackle was closer now to a snarl. 'How was they dressed? Lotta grey around? Military-lookin' men?'

'Yeah. You could say that.' Jubal was now as intrigued as he was wary. 'They mostly wore grey, from what I could see. Like I said, everyone was dead by the time I arrived and there wasn't too much left of anyone.'

'An' the others?'

'Soldiers. Blue-coats looking for a gun-runner.'

It seemed like the right answer because the buffalo gun shifted down from his face to point at his chest as a long sigh broke from between the sun-dried lips.

'How long back?'

'The train was three days, like I told you,' said Jubal. 'The Cavalry was this morning.'

The old man grunted, whether in disgust or anticipation it was impossible to tell, but he shifted slightly, moving his hickory peg around to a more comfortable position.

'So the blue-boys was out after the wagon train, yeh?'

Jubal nodded his assent. 'That's what they said.'

'But they ain't gonna catch it because the injuns got it first.' A note of urgency sounded in the dust-dry voice.

'No. It was finished. The Apaches saw to that.'

'What did you see?' The oldster grinned like a leering death-mask. 'You see a man with white hair an' skin to match? Man as looked like the sun took him up an' bleached his soul? You see anyone like that?'

'No.' Jubal shook his head. 'There wasn't anyone like that.'

19

It was obviously the right answer, because the hammer of the buffalo gun went down and the old man stood up, hopping on his wooden leg.

Like a broken-legged bird, he danced around in a wide-swinging circle, waving his rifle crazily at the sky, laughing and shouting as he went.

'He weren't there! I got him yet. I got him yet. Yahheeee!'

Jubal sat back watching the mad capering as he reached for the Spencer. Even though he appeared to be temporarily exoncrated from the oldster's catalogue of blame he was not prepared to take chances on a wild man's whim; if necessary, he would kill the old man. None the less, he was fascinated. He wanted to know why the cavorting figure was so interested in the journeyings of travellers, and who was the white-haired quarry the man was hunting. So he stayed where he was, simply pulling the Spencer over and levelling it on the old man with the hammer back, ready to fire.

The oldster spotted the movement as the converted carbine shifted over to level on his chest.

'Hell, son,' he giggled, ignoring the dangerous implication of Jubal's weapon, 'ain't no need for that now. You told me what I wanted, so you're all right.'

'Guess so,' Jubal grinned in reply, 'but just to set my mind at rest how about dropping that buffalo gun?'

'This?' The bearded man threw the rifle off to one side. 'Don't hardly need it, anyways.'

He seemed utterly oblivious to the threat of the rifle pointed at his chest as he stopped his capering to fix manic blue eyes on Jubal's face.

'Leastways, not when I got ole Strife pointed at yore back.'

He giggled again, raising the short hairs along Jubal's spine. It was the oldest trick in the world, this side of a whore's come-on, but somehow, when it came from those dried-out, crazy lips, it carried authority and Jubal was suddenly conscious of added danger.

Justification of the prickling down his back came seconds later, hot and wet on the back of his neck.

'Don't move, son.' The old man was showing his blackened teeth in a broad smile. 'Strife mightn't like it. An' if he don't, you're dead.'

Jubal had no way of telling who – or what – was behind him. All he did know was that something was there, breathing fetid air in short gasps that sounded as though the breather was over-eager to kill. Cursing silently, he obeyed the oldster's order to drop the Spencer.

'That's good,' grinned the silver-bearded face, 'now we're even, so I guess I'll introduce you to Strife.'

He clicked his fingers, motioning to his side as Jubal sat very still, conscious of something moving past him with an even, steady tread.

'Meet Strife, friend Jubal.'

Jubal shifted back involuntarily as he looked at the biggest, blackest dog he had ever seen. As warped and gnarled as its master, the animal crouched on powerful haunches, wide-lipped jaws dribbling saliva over curving, yellow teeth that looked like they could rip Jubal's throat out in one bite. Red-rimmed eyes stared unwinkingly from under grey-tinged hair, stilling Jubal more effectively than even a gun.

The dog was ugly. It was near as big as a small pony and looked infinitely more deadly, black and evil like some crouching, momentarily-controlled demon, held back only by the casual hand ruffling the matted hair of its neck.

The oldster chuckled, enjoying the tension.

'Don't worry, friend Jubal. You answered the questions right, so you're home free. I just wanted to make a point clear.'

'Good.' Jubal tried to keep his voice even beneath the red stare of the dog. 'So how about calling that thing off?'

'Ole Strife?' Amusement sounded in the reply. 'He wouldn't hurt you. Less'n I told him to. Course, if I did, he'd tear a little guy like you up in about two bites. Point is not to make me tell him to. Yeh?'

Jubal nodded mute agreement, watching the giant dog settle watchfully on his haunches.

'Yeah. You made your point. I don't have a dog's chance.'

'Right.' The old man cackled, exposing gapped gums. 'You keep that in mind an' you an' me, we'll get along real fine.'

He stepped across to retrieve the Sharps, not bothering to watch Jubal as the younger man sat stock-still beneath the baleful gaze of the giant mastiff. It was impossible to tell how many breeds had gone into its making; wolfhound, certainly, for it had the huge, lean form of those Irish killer dogs, but other breeds too, bulking it out to enormous size, muscling its body and spreading its jaws into gaping, ivory-lined, mantraps. Whatever its ancestry, it sat like a machine of pure destruction, panting in the heat and seeming to wait for the order to kill.

Jubal looked at the dripping teeth and decided not to try for the Spencer.

Discretion proved the better part of valour, for the old man turned around, grinning, and motioned for Jubal to rise.

'Stand up, son.' He held the buffalo gun pointed down with the casual ease of a man who could shift it and fire without too much trouble. 'I got no quarrel with you. Just wanted some information. You give me that, so like I said, you're home free.'

Jubal stood up slowly, his eyes still on the big dog. 'Thanks. Mind if I ask you a couple of questions?'

'Ask away, boy. Ain't gonna promise to answer, but you ask all you want.'

'First off,' said Jubal as casually as he could manage, 'how far is it to Albuquerque?'

'Half a day, no more.' The oldster was friendly now. 'I'm headin' that way. Lead you in if you want.'

'Thanks.' Jubal grinned briefly as he picked up his rifle. 'But what about this man you're looking for?'

The grizzled old-timer smiled evilly, his face shifting from the casual friendship he had shown there to something malignant and dangerous.

'I might tell you one day. Right now you jest remember if'n you see a man all white, like a nigger's black, me an' Strife ain't gonna be far behind. So don't get betwixt us, 'cause if you do I might have to push you outta the way.'

Jubal didn't push the question. It didn't seem worth it after looking at the death's-head grinning at him. Instead he asked the man's name.

'Ahab. Funny name, ain't it?' The old man moved towards his horse as he spoke. 'My daddy was a whaling man, used to know a harpooner by that name. Kinda curious, though, seein' as I was born in Georgia.'

Jubal watched him hook his left foot into the stirrup and lift the wooden peg over the saddle as he spoke. When the pony shifted around, he was able to see that the right stirrup was a heavy metal tube, hammered into a cylindrical shape to accommodate the peg that formed Ahab's right leg.

'Guess it was the influence of his buddy,' continued the one-legged man. 'Some kinda story-writer, as I recall, always spoutin' about whales an' things. Said he was gonna write a book about it with a whaling man called Ahab as captain of the ship. My daddy said he named me for that.'

Jubal knew nothing about the whaling industry and even less about book writers, but he was anxious to keep the old man happy, so he asked, as he climbed astride his own horse, what Ahab's father had been called.

'Helluva lot o' things, depending on who called him,' grinned the oldster, 'but his given name was Ishmael. We was a biblical kinda family.'

He rapped the stump of his wooden leg against the horse's flank, steering it out from the mesquite thicket on to the trail with the dog loping easily at his side. Jubal followed them out, bringing his own mount up to side Ahab's as they cantered through the cooling afternoon towards Albuquerque. He was no wiser about the strange old man than when he had first seen the Sharps pointed at his head, but he was used to the eccentric characters of the West by now, and if Ahab could lead him into town, then he was happy to ride along.

The old man was right about the distance, for they came in sight of Albuquerque early the next morning. The night's camp had been uneasy, with Strife prowling across the desert land, howling and yowling whenever he came on to a slinking coyote. Jubal had got used to the desert dogs moving through the night; they rarely plucked up sufficient courage to come close to a campfire, and if they did, a shout or a shot would drive them off. So he took little notice.

The sound, though, of a coyote plucked up between Strife's massive jaws and killed was unnerving. Three times during the night he heard screams as the big dog killed. Ahab dismissed it easily.

'Hell,' he grinned, enjoying Jubal's reaction, 'he's gotta eat, don't he?'

Jubal knew the logic was right, but the sound of breaking bones and the soggy noise of ripping flesh that came eerily out of the warm night made him uncomfortable. There was something macabre about the strange pair, crippled man and ugly dog, that set his nerves on edge. Ahab had consistently refused to talk any more about the albino he was hunting, but it had become obvious through the afternoon and night spent on the trail that the white-skinned man was the central focus of his life. Jubal could not help wondering what it was that had rendered Ahab so implacable an enemy of the albino.

Or, to some extent, feeling sorry for the quarry hunted by a duo like Ahab and Strife. So the sight of Albuquerque looming on the horizon was welcome, not only for the comfort offered by the hotels located there, but also for the opportunity of fresh company, of respite from the silence of the silver-bearded man and his savage dog.

The town came up high and wide out of the dusty desert landscape. Set squat and solid alongside the slow-flowing Rio Grande, it offered a curiously substantial appearance for all its high-framed, wood-fronted architecture. The cactus-studded desertland broke and cleared a mile out from the first straggle of outlying buildings, scrub giving way to civilization as the trail edged into the city. Buildings stood two, and sometimes three or four, storeys high; smoke, peaceful this time, curled high above the prairie; river-boats sat low and dark on the water, reminding Jubal of his last visit to St. Louis.* He watched the town as they rode in, his skin anticipating a hot bath; his stomach, a hot meal.

* See Jubal Cade – *The Burning Man.*

And, according to Tyree, the mysterious Canfield was down there somewhere. He could deliver the message – whatever it was – and head out on the train, his conscience clear and Ahab and his dog left behind.

Beside him, the old man laughed, the dry-voiced cackle prompting his dog to bark an accompaniment. Jubal turned away from his contemplation of the riverside town to look at Ahab.

'Kinda big, ain't she?' he chuckled. 'A feller could hide hisself down there better'n in the badlands.' A thoughtful look creased his lined face still more, narrowing his pale eyes to near-hidden slits. 'Less'n he stood out, o' course. Like a man with white hair and white skin would.'

A wolfish smile spread across his lips as he eyed the tight-bunched buildings ahead, its sheer malevolence somehow communicating itself to the dog. Like his master, Strife bared yellow teeth in a silent snarl that looked as though he was ready to start hunting through the streets for their quarry. Which was, Jubal thought, most likely exactly what they would do. Ahab was crazy enough.

As he watched the old man, he saw him lift his arm absently to the brim of his sombrero. He pulled the hat off his head and drew a stained shirt sleeve over his damp forehead.

And Jubal's mouth gaped open. He had seen wounds, inflicted them and sewn them up, seen men die in a variety of ways; but he had never seen a man walking around with the front of his scalp missing. Now he knew why no hair showed above Ahab's beard: there was none, it had been lifted along with his scalp.

The old man caught Jubal's look and laughed, enjoying the shocked reaction. Leering evilly, he ran his hand over the livid welt circling his skull, stroking the exposed, greyish bone and crusted scar tissue.

'Yeh, that's right, boy. I got my scalp lifted by the Apache a long time back. I was scoutin' around Juarez when the bastards jumped me an' took the hair.' He giggled in crazy remembrance. 'Couldn't hardly see fer the blood, but I trailed

25

them the next three days. Killed 'em one by one. They died, all I lost was some hair.'

Jubal studied the mess of Ahab's scalp.

'Hair today,' he murmured, 'and gone tomorrow.'

## CHAPTER THREE

Ahab settled the sombrero firmly on his glistening scalp and grunted a command to his horse. Sided by the loping figure of Strife, the pony threw itself into a canter, obviously long-used to its master's commands. Jubal watched the strange old man for a moment, then spurred his own animal down the trail after him. They rode side by side until the buildings of Albuquerque were bulking up high enough to block out the rise of the bluffs on the western bank of the Rio Grande, then Ahab slowed his mount to a walk.

'Jubal,' he remarked casually, 'we'll be partin' now. Like I tole you, I gotta man I want to see, an' I don't want no one else around when we meet. I'd be obliged if you'd rein in a while an' not follow me.'

His right hand was casually stroking the stock of the buffalo gun as he spoke: Jubal took the hint.

He sat the black as Ahab and the dog disappeared between the outlying buildings. The road in wound its way through the outskirts, so that the man and his ugly canine companion were quickly lost to sight amongst the storage sheds and company offices stretching from the riverbank out to the dusty wasteland surrounding the township.

Jubal watched them go, wondering where he might find Canfield and how to go about it. The logical method would be to find the marshal's office and begin asking there, but, so far as possible, he preferred to leave the law out of his present quest. He shrugged and consulted the gold hunter tucked into his vest; the solid-feeling timepiece showed late afternoon and Jubal decided to move into town and find a place to stay. He walked his pony gently between the wooden structures that formed the demarcation line between desert and civilization, studying the marker boards identifying the various buildings as he went. They itemized river-boat offices and warehousing outfits, chandlers and grain merchants; occasionally a small storefront advertised hardware or dry goods, jostling for space between the larger emporiums; boatwrights and blacksmiths showed in abundance, almost as numerous as the larger commercial establishments. In aggregate, they added up to a thriving riverside community, broken every once in a while by cattle pens set close to the river where boats could come in to load.

Farther in, the business premises gave way to houses and hotels and saloons. Off to the western side, lying between the centre of town and the riverbank, Jubal spotted a red light district, the flickering lanterns and tinkling pianos reminding him of Rosie's place in Laredo.* He moved on past as dusk began to settle, heading slowly for the centre of the city.

Although the central area was clearly more respectable than the outskirts, the essential tenor changed little. The saloons were bigger and better-lit, the stores carried lamps in the windows where the others had been dark, but the guns and shovels and saddles displayed behind the glass were the same. Milliners and haberdashers flanked the more mundane emporiums of frontier America, and once Jubal spotted a sign advertising piano lessons. He wondered briefly how the place survived and who its pupils were. Then he saw a stable and turned the horse's head off to the left of the hard-packed street. The big barn-like structure was positioned between a grocery store and a dress shop, the lantern-lit entrance redolent of horse sweat and straw, an old man dragging his grey-flecked beard on his chest as he dozed on a chair in front. He came awake as Jubal walked the black up to the entrance.

'Howdy, mister,' he grinned, showing a mouthful of gum naked of ivory, 'you want to put him up?'

'I guess,' Jubal answered, 'how much?'

'Fifty cents gets you a stall an' hay. Fifty more, an' I'll curry him so you're ridin' a new pony come morning.'

Jubal climbed gratefully out of the saddle and tossed a silver dollar through the air. With surprising agility, the oldster snatched the spinning coin from the air.

* See Jubal Cade – *Killer Silver.*

28

'You got it done, friend. You won't recognize him tomorrow.'

'I may be around a while longer,' remarked Jubal as he pulled his jacket on. 'Depending on a few things.'

'Like what?' The hostler could sense more money in the question.

'On finding someone.' Jubal unbuckled the twin saddlebags and draped them over his left shoulder. 'Maybe you can point me in the right direction.' He reached into his pants pocket as he spoke, getting another dollar ready.

'Depends, mister. Depends.'

Jubal threw the second coin and saw it snatched up with equal agility.

'I'm looking for a man called Canfield. You know anyone of that name?'

'Well now,' the man scratched his grizzled beard, 'seems to me I heard that name a few times.'

Jubal wondered if his task was going to be easy; easy enough to get done that night so he could head for St. Louis come morning.

'It 'pears to me I heard that name a bit around here. There's Ben Canfield runs the bank on main street, an' his boy, Jody; he's got a shipping office on the river. Then there's Logan Canfield – the *Reverend* Logan Canfield, I should say. He runs the Presbyterian mission out on Alamo Road. Then again, I heard of a gambler called Canfield working a faro game in the Square Deal. That a dollar's worth?'

'Yeah. I guess so,' grinned Jubal as he hauled the Spencer off the saddle. 'How about throwing in a place to stay?'

'No trouble,' the oldster called back over his shoulder as he led the black horse into the stable. 'Right next door to the Square Deal. Harve Johnson's rooming house. It's the cleanest, cheapest place in all of Albuquerque. You tell him ole Brian sent you, that'll get you special rates.'

'You related by any chance?' enquired Jubal.

'How'd you guess?' came the reply. 'I married his sister. My name's Levy.'

Jubal grinned and walked away up the street. He had

spotted the saloon mentioned by Levy on his way in, a big, opulent place that looked like it might well offer a satisfying game of poker. If there was a gambler called Canfield working there, it was as good a place as any to start filling out his deal with Tyree, and if a decent rooming house lay next door, then all the better.

He checked into the hotel first. It was small and relatively quiet, Harve Johnson showing him up two flights of carpeted stairs to a room looking out over a stockyard where horses snickered softly in the darkness. It was small, but clean, equipped with a bed that was freshly made and a washstand; it cost a dollar a day with breakfast thrown in and women banned from the rooms.

'Kile Brandstat don't like to let the bawdy houses spread into town-proper,' explained Johnson, 'he worked with Earp up around Wichita an' he always says that you can't give the cat houses a green light or they'll be all over.'

Jubal wasn't interested in the whores anyway, and the news that the rooming house would probably be quiet was good. He was tired. Before sleep, however, he wanted to eat and find the gambler called Canfield.

According to Johnson, the two could be combined as the Square Deal offered food along with its gambling tables and girls.

Jubal waited until the proprietor had left the room, then stashed the two oilskin packages under the mattress and pushed his saddlebags far back behind the clothes closet. Neither hiding place was particularly effective for the amount of money he was carrying, but they were all that were available short of finding a lock-up safe, which would advertise his wealth. He locked the door and headed for the saloon.

Inside, the place was as big and brash and bawdy as it appeared from the street. A solid wall of sound blasted cacophonically against Jubal's eardrums as he pushed through the swing doors. Partly, it came from the piano, two guitars and the banjo jangling a raucous accompaniment to the six fly-blown women displaying flabby, white thighs above the net-stockinged legs they were kicking in the air on a small stage

30

that afforded them a degree of safety from the customers as small as the rostrum they danced on. A greater degree of safety was offered by the two bouncers standing on either side of the stage. Not that their presence deterred the drunker members of the audience from attempting a closer inspection of the women. Their yells, as they were propelled bodily back on to the sawdust-covered floor, added to the din.

Closer to the door, a single piano surrounded by a group of yodelling cowboys sounding more like coyotes than the prairie dogs themselves, set up a rival riot.

In between, drinkers and cardplayers shouted at harassed waiters; three roulette wheels spun and clicked as the little silver balls decided fate and fortunes; and two big fortune wheels whirled mindless coloured circles. Four dice games were in progress and at least five tables were taking money from twist-card players.

Two long bars flanked either side of the smoke-filled room and scarlet-robed women shifted amongst the drinkers, their movements watched – along with all the others – by the shotgun guards spaced around the saloon.

Instinctively, Jubal checked their positions as he moved towards the right-hand bar. There were seven men seated on high stools spread around the room, each one resting with casual tension on his chair, sawn-off, two-barrel Remingtons across their knees.

At the far end, located in a separate room that was partially screened from the main saloon, Jubal spotted the dining area.

He pushed through the crowd, feeling saliva dampen his mouth as he caught the odour of steak over the smoke and sweat. It took him a long time to fight his way through the drinkers, but he made it to the restaurant and found an empty table, where a tired-looking waitress pushed a hand-lettered menu at him. He ordered a T-bone with greens and fries, hot biscuits and, when he had got over the surprise, a bottle of red wine from the list clumsily printed on the reverse side of the menu.

The smaller room was only half-filled and after a cursory glance, the other diners ignored Jubal. He checked them over casually, then settled down to eat; he was hungrier than he had thought and he decided to enjoy his food before seeking out Canfield.

As the evening grew older the saloon became even more crowded, the din rising in volume with each new influx of patrons. Cowboys and storekeepers jostled for space at the two long bars, rubbing shoulders with frock-coated gamblers and blue-shirted soldiers. A platoon of harassed barkeeps kept the shot glasses of whisky and white-headed mugs of beer moving across the polished zinc surfaces as waiters performed acrobatic tricks in their dodging through the crowd with loaded trays. The saloon girls shifted, with scarlet smiles, amongst the drinkers, dropping on to a knee here, wheedling a drink from a customer there. Jubal watched it all from his chair in the dining-room, leaning back comfortably as he finished the last of the wine and lit a cheroot. He inhaled the aromatic smoke, enjoying the taste of nicotine in his mouth, and thought about finding a poker game.

First, though, he wanted the gambler called Canfield.

He collected the tab for the meal and paid the waitress, who looked grateful to have one less customer, then moved out into the main room. He ordered a whiskey at the bar and asked the florid-faced barman where he could find Canfield.

'Zach?' grunted the man. 'He's running a game of five an' wild. Took over when Clayton went sick.'

Jubal wasn't interested in the reasons why Canfield was playing five card poker instead of faro, but it took the angry demands of a thirsty cowpoke, backed up with a promise to introduce the barkeep to an impossible contortion if he didn't hustle a bottle over, before he could obtain Canfield's location. He was glad the sick Clayton wasn't around; it sounded like the man needed a doctor.

Nursing his whiskey – Jubal had never believed in mixing alcohol with cards – he headed for a table in the centre of the room.

Four men handling cards with practised ease were seated around a small, baize-covered oval. Two of them were well into middle-age, showing flecks of grey along their temples, and dressed like businessmen in three-piece dun suits. The third player was a youngster wearing an old, but clean, denim shirt over a pair of well-worn levis encircled by a brown leather gun-belt. The holster was tied down to his thigh, so that the sanded butt of a McFadden single-action ·44 stuck out where he could reach it fast. He was sweating a good deal, and was obviously angry with the fourth man.

Across the table sat an even younger man dressed in a startlingly white suit, a calm smile decorating his beardless baby-face. His calm was fuelling the other's anger and as Jubal came up to the table, it boiled over.

'Fuck it, Canfield,' he snarled, 'there ain't no one draws five aces in five hands. No one.'

'I hate to correct you, Buck.' The voice was as calm as the man's smile, a southern drawl that carried the accents of education in its soft tones, 'but I just did. It's improbable, I admit. But,' a colder, dangerous note entered his voice, 'I do not cheat. And few people accuse me of it.'

He kept both hands in clear view on the table as he spoke, manicured nails resting on either side of an ace-high straight, and Jubal wondered where he hung his gun, because it was obvious he would need one very soon.

The moment came fast and mean as Buck stood up, kicking his chair back as his thumb flicked the safety loop off the hammer of the McFadden. The big gun seemed to jump into his hand with the same movement that brought him to his feet. He was fast, as fast as anyone Jubal had seen, and he waited for the explosion of blood from Canfield's snow-white shirt front.

But fast as Buck drew, he was too slow to beat the flash of silver that hurtled across the three feet separating him from the gambler. The McFadden detonated with a thunderous roar that ploughed a bullet into and through the tabletop, sending cards flying in wild spirals through the smoke-filled air. The youngster gagged, his face purpling with the useless effort of sucking oxygen into his lungs as his left hand rose to clutch at the hilt of the knife protruding from the base of his throat. He coughed blood and tried to lift the ·44 for a second shot as his eyes began to glaze and the horrible knowledge of his own death registered in his mind. But Canfield was on his feet too, moving delicately to one side to avoid the blood pumping from Buck's neck as he grabbed the boy's wrist, pushing the gun down so that the bullet hit the floor.

Then Buck's knees gave way and he pitched forwards, bounced off the edge of the table, and collapsed on to the floor.

Canfield moved around the table to squat beside the corpse. Carefully, he pulled the knife free and wiped the blade on Buck's shirt. Then he pressed a button and folded the blade back into the hilt before shoving the switchblade into a sheath hidden beneath his right sleeve.

'A fair fight, I believe,' he remarked casually to the older players. 'I trust that you gentlemen will bear witness to that fact.'

It sounded more like a statement than a question; the other two nodded silent agreement, avoiding Canfield's eyes.

'Good. Then let's play cards.' The gambler sat down as a bouncer, cradling his scattergun in his right elbow, pushed through the crowd, dragging the corpse behind him.

Jubal moved up closer to the table.

'I guess you got room for a fourth?' he enquired.

Canfield smiled, studying Jubal's face. 'Yes, indeed. We now have room for a fourth. Sit down, mister...?'

'Cade,' replied Jubal. 'Doctor, though, not mister. Doctor Jubal Cade.'

'Sit down, Doctor Cade.' Canfield's composure was total. 'Had you arrived a little earlier, young Buck might have used your professional services.'

'I doubt it,' Jubal answered, looking directly at the gambler, 'he looked pretty choked off to me.'

'Yes,' Canfield's smile remained casually pleasant. 'I believe he got the point of my argument. However, permit me to introduce myself: Zachariah T. Canfield, at your service.' He gestured to the man on his right. 'My namesake, Ben Canfield, worthy president of our leading bank. And Joshua Kilmane,

34

owner of the stockyards you doubtless noticed coming into town.'

Jubal nodded his greetings, grateful that he had tipped four hundred dollars in notes and coin into his pockets before leaving the rooming house. This had all the earmarks of an expensive game. Not that it worried him unduly: he was too good a cardplayer to be daunted by high stakes. What did perturb him slightly was the presence of two Canfields at the table. Somehow he would have to either broach the subject of Tyree's message to both of them, or engineer individual meetings. The former course was, he decided, the best for the simple reason that it would save time. Right now, though, he was going to play cards.

'The game,' Canfield explained, 'is five card draw with dealer calling the wild cards. Aces are high and the minimum bet is two dollars.'

Jubal grinned his agreement as Canfield cut a fresh pack and drew a wad of notes from the inside pocket of his jacket. They were mostly fives and tens, and when he saw the other three toss two dollars apiece on to the table, he dropped a five on to the coins and extracted three dollars change. With a standing pot of eight dollars a hand, the game was worth playing even with poor cards.

Canfield handed the pack to Kilmane who called threes as wild and dealt with a three-and-two pattern. It was up to Jubal to open and he pushed two dollars forwards, hoping to give his pair of sevens some stablemates. He stayed in for another five dollars purely to assess his opponents, then folded before Ben Canfield took a fifty-seven dollar pot with three fours and a pair of eights. The cards came to Jubal and he dealt straight, each player getting a card in turn. He left his own hand face down as he announced deuces wild then turned the cards up to discover three twos and an ace. It was unbelievable luck, and Jubal was abruptly conscious of the switchblade in Zachariah Canfield's cuff. Academically, he wondered if he could draw and fire the Colt holstered beneath his jacket before the knife hit him.

The change round gave him a ten, same suit as the ace, and

he came out of the hand one hundred and fifty dollars better off. Canfield grinned ruefully, flicking a non-existent speck of dust from his cuff.

'Doctor,' he murmured, 'I believe I've found an opponent worthy of the game.'

Jubal smiled, pushing his cards over to Ben Canfield. The banker gathered up the deck and began to deal.

'Fives are wild.'

His florid face showed evidence of his sedentary occupation, and the slight twist of his thick lips indicated a poor hand. Jubal noticed the tiny grimace as he studied his own hand. He had drawn a pair of queens, and a six, nine and jack. He held the jack and changed two, picking up a ten and a three. The two Canfields dropped out and Jubal bluffed Kilmane up to a thirty dollar pot before the cattle dealer folded.

He lost the next two hands, then won three in succession, raising his initial four hundred dollar stake to seven hundred and fifty-four before Kilmane announced his intention of returning to his wife and family. He was, Jubal calculated, at least two hundred dollars down on the game. Not that it seemed to bother him.

'Forgive me, gentlemen,' he said as he rose, 'but the little lady'll be wondering where I am.' The others laughed with him as he said it. 'Another time I'll get my revenge.'

Ben Canfield suggested a rest and called for whiskey as Kilmane departed. No one else wanted to sit in, so the three men sat back in their chairs, relaxing as Canfield poured the drinks. Jubal refused the offer. Poker demanded concentration, which alcohol fuzzed; the only thing that mattered was the hand in front of you and the other players. To concern yourself with any peripheral activities was the action of a man with no sense, or one who did not care if he lost. Jubal was neither.

Still sipping his original drink, he began, tentatively, to question the two Canfields.

Ben Canfield had been born in Washington, the son of a minor government official and a society lady. Tired of his parents' bickering, he had headed west when he was only fifteen, working his way over the wilderness trail to California.

He had been there before the Forty-Niners and made a small fortune trading in dry goods and hardware. After the strikes dried up, he had transferred his interests to land. And made more money. At twenty-nine he was a rich man. In 1861, aged thirty-three, he had read a despatch about the Battle of First Bull Run. Immediately, he cashed in his assets, freed the slaves he owned, and set out on the trail eastwards. Half a year later he was a captain in the 9th New York Cavalry. When the bloody conflict ended at Appomattox four years later, he was a colonel. After the peace was signed, he had refused a permanent commission and headed west again. Albuquerque had looked like a growing town, so he had stopped there, bought into the bank and swiftly found himself made its president.

He was not the Canfield Jubal sought.

The white-suited gambler, on the other hand, could easily be the man Tyree had meant. He did not disclose his age, but Jubal guessed that he would have been about seventeen when the Civil War ended; old enough to have seen action. And he was a Southerner from Georgia, though reticent about his past.

As they commenced the game again, Jubal concentrated on poker and discreet probing.

'I met a Southerner riding in,' he remarked as Canfield dealt cards. 'Man called Tyree.'

'Common enough name,' murmured Canfield. 'You taking cards, Ben?'

The banker changed three; Jubal only one: he was holding a pair of tens and two fives and picked up a wild seven to fill a full house.

He took a seventy dollar pot and waited until Ben Canfield was dealing before he spoke again.

'Said he knew a man named Canfield in Albuquerque,' he remarked casually.

'There's more than the two of us,' said Zachariah, picking up his cards.

'Sure is,' agreed the banker, 'my boy Jody for starters. Though he's not likely to be the one. Only came out here from college a year ago, an' right now he's in El Paso setting up a cattle deal. Two cards, please, Zach.'

The gambler fed cards, Canfield's two and two more for Jubal. Nothing came out of either the change round or the conversation and Jubal dumped his hand as the talking died. The pot went to the younger Canfield and as he scooped up his winnings, Jubal resumed his casual chatter.

'Any others? I'd like to fill a promise.'

'Just now, Doctor,' said Zachariah evenly, 'you can fill your promise to deal cards.'

Jubal took the hint and spread cards with deft movements around the table. He called deuces wild again, calculating that it was about time they showed up as the pack had remained unshuffled since Buck's sudden departure from the game.

His memory for cards paid off in the shape of a two, though – he reminded himself – that could easily mean the others had twos as well, and a pair of kings. The gambler changed two cards, the banker three, and Jubal two. His change cards gave him a six and a four and the twitch on Ben Canfield's face the knowledge that the banker had nothing. The round ended in a stand off between Jubal and Zachariah Canfield with the white-suited man paying twenty-six dollars to see Jubal's hand.

It was a long shot that missed. Canfield took the pot, reducing Jubal's winnings by thirty-eight dollars. It still left him several hundred ahead of his starting stake, but losing was a thing with no appeal to Jubal and for the next few rounds he forgot his mission and concentrated on winning.

It paid off, for round midnight Ben Canfield threw in his cards and decided to go home.

'A pleasant evening,' he said, pushing back his chair, 'though the bank rate may have go to up as a result. Thank you, gentlemen. I'll see you again, Zach; and you, I hope, Doctor Cade.'

'I hope so,' answered Jubal politely. 'If not, thank you for the game.'

The banker murmured something about pleasant company and good cards and made his way through the crowd, only slightly thinned by the late hour.

As he pushed his way out of the saloon, Zachariah suggested

that they end the game and have a drink. The last few hands had boosted Jubal's winnings to around nine hundred dollars, which, added to the gold stashed in his room, would keep Andy Prescott in the Lenz Clinic for several months,* so he was happy now to ease up and see what he could find out about whichever Canfield he was looking for. If the man really was in Albuquerque.

At the bar they ordered whiskey, Jubal waiting for Canfield to speak.

'So, Doctor,' the gambler broke the silence, 'you're looking for a man called Canfield.'

'Yeah,' Jubal sipped his drink, 'like I said, I met a man called Tyree who asked me to take a message. I made him a promise and I'd like to keep it.'

'Admirable,' nodded the young gambler, 'my brother would approve of so noble a sentiment.'

'Your brother?' Jubal was curious.

'Indeed, Doctor. My brother. The overly reverend Logan Canfield.'

'Maybe he's the one Tyree meant,' suggested Jubal.

'It's possible,' agreed Canfield. 'He has, if anything, a circle of acquaintances both wider and odder than my own.'

'Perhaps I should meet him,' said Jubal.

'Perhaps you should,' Canfield agreed, 'for the only Tyree I ever knew was a galloper with the Union cavalry. A remarkable horseman who rode with a man called Ford. I met them both at Fort Apache on the Rio Grande.'

'Doesn't sound like the Tyree I met,' said Jubal. 'He was a Southerner, like yourself.'

'In that case,' Canfield murmured, emptying his glass, 'you must meet my brother. He retains his ties with the South far more than do I.'

'Can you introduce me?' Jubal wondered, even though he sensed a tension existed between the unlikely brothers.

'Certainly,' smiled the gambler, 'Logan would welcome the chance to save your soul as avidly as he does mine.'

'It's not my soul I'm interested in,' grinned Jubal, ordering

* See Jubal Cade – *Double Cross*.

two fresh whiskies. 'Just delivering the message.'

'Logan,' muttered Canfield, 'is always interested in placing souls with the Great Fisherman, although he does tend to flounder when he's not perched in his pulpit.'

# CHAPTER FOUR

Logan Canfield was one hell of a preacher. Jubal found that out the next day, when Zachariah took him along to the mission on the Alamo Road. They slipped quietly into the single-storey wooden building, unnoticed in the crowd of worshippers now that the gambler had changed his white suit for a more sober grey affair. They found places on the roughly hewn benches towards the rear of the church and settled down to listen to the preacher. Two hymns were sung and three prayers offered up before Logan Canfield mounted the ornately carved pulpit that dominated the mission. Standing ten feet above his congregation, his hands rested on the carved heads of huge-beaked eagles, he was an impressive figure, commanding the total attention of his parishioners as he began, in a sonorous voice that echoed off the farthest reaches of the church, to deliver his sermon.

'Our message this day,' the voice roared like muted thunder over the heads of the listeners, 'is taken from the book of Jeremiah, who struggled against the enemies of Israel, righteous and mighty in his sure strength.'

He paused, blazing blue eyes surveying the awestruck faces below him, seeming to probe deep into the souls of all.

'And yet, my friends, even Jeremiah doubted the strength of his faith, seeking to refuse his divine mission. And so it was that the Lord said unto Jeremiah, "*thou shalt go to all that I shall send thee, and whatsoever I command thee thou shalt speak. Be not afraid of their faces: for I am with thee to deliver thee, saith the Lord.*" And even so, brethren, is it with us, even here in this wilderness where men forget God for their guns, forsake the Good Book for a deck of cards.'

Zachariah winked at Jubal as his brother's words rolled around the mission hall.

'But what else did the Lord say?' Canfield demanded. 'I tell

41

you, friends, He said, *"I have this day set thee over the nations and over the kingdoms, to root out, and to pull down, and to destroy, and to throw down, to build, and to plant."* That is what He said. And so shall we do here, in this sin-ridden city of Albuquerque, where the minions of the Dark One hold sway, though it shall not be for long. For like Jeremiah, so shall we pull down and destroy the temples of the ungodly.'

The sermon continued as Jubal studied the preacher's face. The man was either inspired or a fanatic, but there was no denying the power of his oratory. He held the crowd in the palm of his hand, his words moving them like the strings on a puppet.

He was the focal point of the whole gathering, not only because of his commanding position on the pulpit and his deep-throated, resonant voice, but also because of his appearance. He was dressed all in black, suit sitting tight over black-shirted chest, the sombre colour broken only by the patch of white at his throat. The black threw up the deep tan of his face and the gleaming mane of silver hair that flowed down over his collar. He looked, thought Jubal, like the popular conception of an Old Testament prophet: big, brawny and handsome. It was an idea clearly shared by the women in the congregation, which probably explained why they outnumbered the men by about three to one. They gazed, starry-eyed and open-mouthed, at the Reverend Canfield, drinking in his words as they clutched their bibles in white-knuckling fingers.

Jubal wondered how many came along to services to hear the word of the Lord, and how many to look at the preacher. Whatever their reasons, they gave generously when the collection came round, coins tinkling profitably into the brass pot as Logan Canfield showed even white teeth in a benign smile from his vantage point in the pulpit.

He waited until the collection was taken before announcing the next hymn, a ragged-voiced version of *Gather By The River*, and leading the congregation in a final prayer. Then he descended from the pulpit like Moses coming down the mountain and walked, smiling and nodding pleasantly, down the aisle to the door.

Jubal and Zachariah remained seated as the parishioners rose to leave, filing slowly out of the church past their minister.

A steady hum of conversation marked their passage as they paid their respects to Logan Canfield and the preacher made the right, diplomatic responses.

'Morning, Mrs. Higgins. Hot enough for you?'

'Miss Fraser. Good to see you.'

'Dinner, Mrs. Craig? Why thank you, yes.'

'See you Sunday, Mr. Freeman.'

*'What in the hell are you doing here?'*

Zachariah and Jubal had joined the line of departing worshippers, reaching the preacher as the last of his flock hurried about their ordinary business. He was obviously surprised to see his brother; and not at all pleased.

'Thought I'd drop by and see how business is going,' grinned Zachariah, ignoring the straight-lipped disapproval of his brother.

'My mission is not, as I keep telling you, *business*.' Canfield bit on the words. 'It is a *cause*. Something most probably beyond your comprehension.'

He paused, his measured words a contrast to the spontaneous outburst at first sight of his brother. He had not yet noticed Jubal standing slightly to one side of the door, where shadow partially hid him from view, and was showing signs of irritation and embarrassment as he ushered Zachariah inside. They were unlikely siblings, the baby-faced gambler and the black-clad minister, and there was clearly little love lost between them. Logan appeared relieved when he succeeded in getting Zachariah into the mission building with the door shut behind him. Only then did he notice Jubal, confusion showing on his handsome features.

'Don't worry, brother.' Zachariah was enjoying the scene. 'He's a friend of mine. Wanted to meet you.'

Logan gathered himself up, taking refuge behind his cloth as he fixed Jubal with a pale blue stare.

'Another gambler? A fellow wastrel, wary of an honest day's toil?'

43

'Not quite,' said Jubal evenly. 'I play cards once in a while, but I'm a doctor by profession.'

Logan was taken aback, but swiftly regained his composure. 'A doctor, you say?'

'That's what he said,' Zachariah interposed.

'And what,' the preacher ignored his brother, 'brings you to the mission?'

'A message,' Jubal replied. 'One I promised to deliver to a man named Canfield.'

'My name, certainly,' the minister agreed, 'but also, to my regret, that of my brother. Presumably, though, he is not the man you seek.'

'Logan,' murmured Zachariah, 'you talk too much. If it was me, would I have brought him here?'

Logan nodded his agreement, motioning Jubal to a seat on one of the plank benches.

'Your name, doctor?'

'Cade.' Jubal answered. 'Jubal Cade.'

'Pleased to meet you, Doctor Cade.' They shook hands, Canfield's grip proving as powerful as his appearance suggested. 'And the message?'

Succinctly, Jubal described the burned-out wagon train and Tyree's request that he ride to Albuquerque and tell Canfield about the attack, that Beauregard – whoever he was – would no longer get his guns and cattle. He left out the details of the sealed package: until he was sure of his man he intended to hold that information secret.

No sign of recognition showed on the preacher's aquiline face, though Jubal studied it carefully.

'Why come to me?'

Zachariah answered for Jubal. 'Well, it's not me he's looking for. Ben Canfield's never heard of either Tyree or Beauregard and it's not likely to be Jody, seeing that he's been in El Paso the past few weeks. That leaves you, brother.'

'It leaves me confused,' said Canfield firmly, 'as to why you should think I might have anything to do with a band of gunrunners or two men I've never heard of before. No; I'm sorry, Doctor Cade, but I am not the Canfield you're looking for.'

He rose to his feet.

'Now, if you will excuse me...'

Jubal shrugged. 'Oh well. I did my best for Tyree, so I guess I can ride on now.'

'To where?' Logan Canfield's enquiry was polite and disinterested, the kind of pleasantry a tactful man would make rather than seem anxious to get rid of an unwelcome guest.

'St. Louis,' Jubal said as he walked to the door, 'there are some people there I have to visit.'

'If I don't see you again,' murmured Canfield as he held the door, 'I trust it will be a pleasant journey.'

Jubal smiled polite thanks, his eyes caught by the hand resting on the woodwork of the doorframe. Logan Canfield might be somewhat long-winded in his speech, sounding like a typical drawing-room preacher more used to holding a teacup than a tool, but his hands gave the lie to that impression. They were big and calloused, long, sinewy fingers splaying out from a palm that looked as though it had held work implements aplenty. When he lifted his arm Jubal noticed the telltale marks of a rider etched across the hand, the hardened skin that came from holding a horse's reins. Whatever his manner, Logan Canfield was accustomed to using his hands for more purposes than lifting teacups.

Thoughtfully, Jubal fell into step beside Zachariah.

'How come you two don't get on?' It was a casual-sounding question.

'Never have,' said the gambler shortly, 'not since we were kids.' He grinned. 'Hell, we've not even seen one another in years.

'Logan and I were born in Macon, Georgia. Pa had a plantation there, big place with plenty of slaves and enough cotton growing to keep me in the style to which I've since become accustomed. Logan was the first son, eight years older than me and all set to inherit the old homestead. Then the war came along and we lost everything when Sherman marched through Georgia.'

He fell silent for a while.

'It killed Pa, though I wasn't there to see it. I'd enlisted the

45

year before and got stuck in the siege of Petersburg. Logan was someplace up the Shenandoah. When we both got back there wasn't much left to stay for. The house was burned and the cotton with it, the only things left were the gravestones and the Yankee carpetbaggers parcelling out the land.

'I took one look and rode west. I always was good with cards and work didn't appeal too much, so here I am: a professional gambler.

'Logan stayed on. Tried to get the place back together, but he couldn't. He never forgave me for that, reckoned that we might have done it if I'd stayed on to help him. Instead, he was forced to sell up for practically nothing.

'I didn't see him for a couple of years, then I ran into him in St. Joe. He had a store that was losing money faster than sand in a sieve, so I loaned him some. He never forgave me for that either. Next time we met was in Denver. I was doing well by then, but Logan was skinning mules for the Army and hating every minute of it. Used to take it out on the mules; he was a real killer with a bull-whip.

'We ran across one another a couple more times in Tularosa and Fort Worth, then nothing for about three years.'

Canfield grinned at Jubal as they approached the Square Deal.

'I'd been more or less settled here for the better part of a year. Making money too. Then I heard about the new mission just started up, so I went along to see what it was like. I saw Logan standing in the pulpit spouting fire and brimstone. That was a month or so ago; he still hasn't forgiven me.'

'Not too Christian of him,' Jubal suggested. 'I always thought charity began at home.'

'So far as Logan's concerned,' grinned Zachariah, 'home's gone and I'm the prodigal son.'

'Well, I can't offer you a fatted calf,' said Jubal, 'but I can stake you a dinner. How about it?'

# CHAPTER FIVE

That evening Zach Canfield went back to handling his faro game, so Jubal sat in on a poker session. The Square Deal was a good deal quieter than the previous night, and Jubal realized with a shock of surprise that it was Sunday. The journey across the badlands had stripped all sense of passing time from his conscious mind, so that he drifted through the days without the set routine of work to establish a timetable in his head. For the people of Albuquerque, Saturday night had been the big weekly blow-up, rounded out in traditional frontier fashion with the killing of Buck. Sunday was the quiet time; for the cowboys and soldiers nursing Saturday-night hangovers it was sobering-up day, for the righteous people it was church and family dinner.

For Jubal it was just one more day.

Come Monday, he decided as he dealt cards, he would ride out, heading East. Whichever Canfield he had agreed to contact was either no longer in town, or unwilling to reveal himself. Jubal had done his best to fulfil the promise he had made Tyree and felt clear-conscienced about quitting town with the five hundred dollars in his saddlebags and the sealed message left with the marshal. If the Canfield Tyree had wanted ever materialized, he might find the package; it wasn't Jubal's concern any longer.

He concentrated on the cards, picking up a few dollars more from the other players. One was a cowpoke riding south to Texas after the ranch he had been working in Montana folded. He was chancing his last wage packet on the hope of winning and finding a new job. He was losing. The other two players were both soldiers from the local garrison. One was a grizzled three-striper who played with the cautious knowledge of long years of bunkhouse games backed by the meagre pay of a cavalryman. His companion was a green recruit, his uniform shirt and yellow-striped pants considerably cleaner than his sergeant's. He was losing too.

Jubal was some twenty dollars ahead, with the sergeant nine behind him. After Saturday's game, it was small beer, but Jubal played for the sheer enjoyment; and when he played, it was to win, irrespective of the amount. Poker was a serious game and feeling sorry for a cowboy with busted pockets or a raw horse soldier who barely knew a straight from a flush had no part in the tactics of the contest.

Jubal smiled, showing his broken front teeth in a grin that lifted years off his face as he hauled in a ten dollar pot.

The cowboy, a prematurely aged saddlehand called Kelso, lifted his stained hat to wipe his forehead clear of the loser's sweat. His hair was grey, nearly white even though he could not have been more than thirty. He was watching his grubstake disappear and he was nervous about it.

He dropped the hat on to the table and announced his intention of quitting while he still had enough money left to buy a couple of meals. He surveyed Jubal with light grey eyes surrounded by the wrinkles produced by long hours in the open air.

'You're too damn' good fer me, friend,' he said ruefully, 'so I figger to back out now while I still got a bit left.'

He stood up and walked over to the bar. His whiskey was halfway to his lips when a low-throated growl, full of raw menace, stopped the glass.

Slightly to his left, red lips drawn back to expose yellow fangs, Strife crouched, his huge black body drawn up tight, ready to launch his murderous jaws at Kelso's throat. Behind the big dog stood Ahab, his wooden leg tapping impatiently on the sawdusted floor, his left hand resting lightly on the barrel of the ·50 calibre Sharps lying on the bar. He grinned as Kelso paled.

'Don't worry, friend. The dog just mistook you fer someone else. You ain't got no excuse to get nervous.'

He murmured to the dog, reaching out to stroke the erect hairs along its neck.

Slowly, Strife relaxed, his hackles going down as the tension drained from his lean body. The tension remained in Kelso, showing in the taut lines across his forehead where beads of sweat trickled from under his near-white hair. Thickly, he mouthed a curse.

'Get that fuckin' thing outta here.' His right hand was moving towards the Colt slung on his hip. 'I never could stand dogs.'

'Aw, come on.' Ahab sounded almost apologetic. 'Ole Strife ain't gonna hurt you. Not now. He just took you fer another feller.'

'I don't give a good goddam,' snarled Kelso. 'I don't like dogs, so get the black bastard outta here.'

Jubal had stopped playing cards to watch the scene being played out. Now he murmured his own apologies to the soldiers and rose to walk over to the bar, placing himself equidistant between Ahab and Kelso.

'Hey, c'mon, gents,' he grinned, 'there's no cause for concern, just a mistake on the dog's part. Why not take a drink with me and forget it?'

'Whiskey,' said Ahab.

'Fuck off,' grunted Kelso. 'I cain't stand dogs an' I ain't about to drink with no damn' dog-lover.'

Strife sensed the tension in the air and growled low in his throat as two more cowboys moved up to back Kelso. They had the same weather-beaten look and the same tired, resentful eyes. Like Kelso, they were dressed in faded denim and big Tex-Mex spurs; and they both carried revolvers in well-worn holsters.

'Meet my buddies,' grinned Kelso, confident of winning his point on a three-against-two bet, 'Cantrell an' Cochrane.'

'Why don't we all take a drink?' Jubal asked.

'They don't drink nothin' more'n sarsaparilla,' Kelso grunted. 'So why don't you back off?'

'Maybe I don't want a poker game spoiled' Jubal was beginning to get angry. He wasn't sure why he should try to help Ahab, but he knew that Kelso's attitude was starting to irritate him. 'And maybe I feel that three men against one's not quite fair odds.'

Kelso chose that moment to go for his gun. He was surprisingly fast for a cowboy, but Strife was faster still. The big dog came off the floor of the saloon in a lethal spring that snapped jaws like a man-trap around Kelso's wrist. The cowboy screamed, high and shrill, as he was knocked over backwards by the weight of the dog's body, his gun blasting a hole in the plank floor.

Ahab was slightly slower, so that Cantrell's bullet ripped through the fleshy part of his upper arm before he could level the Sharps. He grimaced, dropping the buffalo gun as he clutched at the bleeding hole in his left arm.

Jubal's Colt was out and pointing at Cantrell as Cochrane's bullet whistled past his head. Without aiming, he shifted the gun and triggered a shot that blew away a chunk of the cowboy's ear. Cochrane yelped and threw himself sideways as he fired again. The shot went wild, but it gave him the time he needed to tip a table on its side and find cover. Cantrell followed suit as Ahab showed surprising agility in his tumble over the bar.

Momentarily alone, Jubal powered himself to one side as bullets spanged over his head. He hit the floor and rolled, kicking chairs aside as he went, until he reached up behind a table. He grabbed the edge and hauled it over, ignoring the glasses and cards that showered around him as bullets hit the wood.

Behind him, he heard Zach Canfield shouting for the shotgun guards to stay out of the fight. Jubal was grateful: seven short-muzzled scatterguns firing in unison would have killed everyone. One guard, more zealous or more bloodthirsty than his companions, ignored Canfield's shout, moving in a zig-zag run across the saloon. A bullet from Cantrell or Cochrane, Jubal couldn't tell which, stopped him in his tracks. The man coughed and staggered, pitching forwards as a big red hole blossomed on his chest. His arms thrust out, the Remington pitching from his lifeless fingers as he died, hurling the gun in Jubal's direction.

It slid across the floor to Jubal's feet and he picked it up, aware of the devastating firepower of the short-barrelled weapon.

Kelso was still wrestling with Strife, battering at the dog's head with his good hand as the great mastiff clung grimly to his wrist. Ahab was crouched at one end of the bar, angling the Sharps around the corner as he looked for a shot. Cantrell and Cochrane were huddled behind their protecting tables as the other occupants of the Square Deal scattered in all directions.

Jubal heard two more shots thud into his own table and decided to take a chance.

He powered himself sideways, hurtling out from behind the woodwork as he triggered the Remington. Both barrels discharged into the table sheltering Cochrane, the heavy pellets blowing the table apart in a spreading confusion of splinters and bloody flesh. Cochrane jumped up, clutching at the mess the spreading shot and flying splinters had made of his face, presenting a clear target to Ahab's Sharps.

The bellow of the ·50 calibre gun filled the saloon with echoing sound. Cochrane was lifted off his feet, flying ten paces backwards as the bullet exited through his back. He dropped his Colt as he flew, hit a table that toppled over as a smear of bright red stained the green baize, and slid to a sitting position against it as the faded blue denim of his shirt front turned crimson.

The Square Deal was momentarily silent, shocked by the naked violence of scattergun and Sharps and sudden death. Jubal took advantage of the lull, rolling on to his stomach and triggering two shots through the table sheltering Cantrell. Both bullets went straight through the wood into the cowboy's skull. The first blew his jaw away, the second stopped the pain because it hit him dead centre of his forehead, drilling through flesh and bone to explode his brain and blast out through the back of his head in a fan of blood-stained grey brain matter.

Ahab saw him die and hopped to his feet. He moved swiftly around the bar, shouting at Strife as he came. The big dog backed off from Kelso so that his master had a clear field of fire. Ahab pushed the muzzle of the buffalo gun into Kelso's mouth.

'So you don't like dogs, huh? See how you like this.'

He squeezed the trigger.

Jubal winced as Kelso's head exploded. His skull flew back under the impact, bouncing on the floor as it disintegrated, spraying blood and bone in a great circle over the planking. Then he felt a hard shove on his back and a cold voice talking in his ear, low and dangerous.

'Don't move, mister, or you're dead.'

He twisted his head around and found himself looking at a six-pointed star pinned on to a black vest. The prodding in his back came from the Colt held, cocked and ready to fire, in the hand of the big, blond man wearing the marshal's badge.

'Name's Brandstat,' said the marshal, 'I'm the law around here an' like I said: you make a wrong move an' you're dead.'

Jubal set his own gun down gently on the floor. Two deputies armed with Winchesters were covering Ahab, who was holding on to Strife's collar to keep the big dog in check.

'It appears to me,' Brandstat went on in the same flat tones, 'that you both got some questions to answer. An' the best place for us to talk is back at the jail. On yore feet.' He motioned with his gun as he spoke.

Jubal rose cautiously to his feet, standing silent as the marshal picked up his Colt and stuck it in his belt. Then, flanked by Ahab and the restlessly growling Strife, he walked out of the saloon surrounded by Brandstat and his deputies.

Zach Canfield tried to protest until a cold stare from the marshal stopped him. Brandstat was, Jubal realized, a man to be reckoned with. Still, there was nothing to be lost in trying to reason with him.

'It was a fair fight, marshal,' he said evenly, 'three of them started it. We just finished it.'

Brandstat's gun dug viciously between Jubal's shoulder-blades.

'Shut up. There's three men dead I don't know, an' one I do. You was part of it an' yore alive. You want to talk, you do it come mornin' in the jail. Until then keep yore mouth shut.'

Jubal shut his mouth and stepped out on to the sidewalk as Brandstat directed. He walked in silence towards the marshal's office until a curse from Ahab caught his attention. The old man was clutching at his wooden leg and swearing softly, bent over so that his face was close to his dog's ear. Brandstat. and his deputies stopped, demanding to know what was the matter.

'My leg.' Ahab's voice carried a totally uncharacteristic pleading note. 'It's my leg. It hurts.'

One of the deputies lowered his rifle and stepped up alongside the oldster. As he did, Ahab brought the hickory peg up in a sweeping arc that connected with the man's chin. The deputy's head snapped back with a solid crunch as the tip of the wooden leg smashed his jaws together. At the same time Strife hurled himself against the second deputy, great jaws clacking shut fractions of an inch from the man's throat. One lawman collapsed unconscious, the other fell back in fright, tripping over his companion so that he stretched his length on the boardwalk.

Only the marshal retained his composure; until Ahab's spinning body smashed Jubal against him. Together they went down in a tumble of flying limbs, Brandstat's gun exploding into the sky. He cursed as he pushed to his knees, triggering shots after the running figures heading fast down a side alley. He got back on to his feet, ordering his conscious deputy to pull himself together and watch Jubal as he ran hard after Ahab and Strife.

Long minutes later he returned, swearing volubly at the loss of his prisoner. Roughly, he pushed Jubal ahead of him towards the jail.

'Yore friend may have gone,' he grunted bitterly, 'but that just means you're in double trouble.'

'Seems to me,' Jubal said bitterly as the cell door closed, 'that a bird in the coop is worth two in the open.'

'Somethin' like that.' Brandstat's voice was cold and evil. 'I got my convictions, an' it looks like you're gonna be one of them.'

# CHAPTER SIX

The cell was no more than ten feet by ten, two sides of solid stone with a single small window barred with struts of rusted iron set high into the back wall. The third side consisted of tall steel struts that cut the cell off from its empty companion cage, while the front was mostly taken up with the door, a cross-barred affair with a big lock set into the frame halfway down.

Brandstat had searched Jubal thoroughly before shoving him into the cell, extracting cartridges and matches from his pockets and checking him for hidden weapons. Now he sat on the pull-down bench bed wondering how he could get out. The marshal had more or less guaranteed a hanging, even though he had to wait four to five weeks before the circuit judge came round.

Jubal didn't want to wait that long, but he could not see any alternative as he studied the solid framework of the cell.

On past the cell door, the square-shaped building opened out to an office. Brandstat sat there now, chair tipped back to let his feet rest on the edge of his cluttered desk. Most of the clutter was paper, wanted posters and personal, lawman-to-lawman, messages; Jubal hoped there was no dodger from Denver: he had an unpleasant feeling that Brandstat might advance the execution to now if he knew money was involved in Jubal's death.

But the big marshal stood up at last, shaking his head as he turned to face his prisoner.

'Looks like you're clean fer the time bein',· Cade.' He sounded sorry as he said it. 'So I guess you just wait there 'til the judge turns up.'

Jubal didn't bother to reply: there didn't seem any point.

The lawman grinned unpleasantly and pulled the wooden door connecting the cells and the outer office shut. Jubal could hear a key turning in the lock, followed by the sound of foot-steps and the outer door closing. Then it was quiet. The jail was too far away from the main establishments of central Albuquerque to pick up much noise, especially on a relatively quiet Sunday night.

With nothing else to do, he settled down to sleep.

When he awoke it was dark, the full black of deep night. Something, though, had brought him up out of slumber and he lay still on the bunk, orienting himself in the darkness as he tried to figure what it was.

Then he knew. The door to the office flew open and a dark figure moved towards the cell. Jubal swung his legs on to the floor, waiting as a key grated in the lock and the barred door swung open.

'Move it.' The voice was harsh with urgency and vaguely familiar. '*Come on*. Kile won't stay asleep for ever and I can't afford to be found out.'

Jubal stood up, moving fast across the cell and through the door. He followed the black-clad man into the marshal's office and saw Kile Brandstat stretched on the floor beside an up-turned chair, a thin trickle of blood flowing from a wound in his scalp.

'He's not dead.' The man turned as he spoke and Jubal knew why the voice had sounded familiar.

It belonged to the Reverend Logan Canfield.

'Pick up your gun and let's go.'

'Sure.' Jubal wasn't about to argue, but together with his Colt and the shoulder holster, he wanted his watch back. He rummaged through Brandstat's desk until he found the gold hunter.

'Dammit to hell, you bastard,' Canfield muttered angrily, 'will you hurry?'

'I want something of mine,' grunted Jubal in the same urgent tone.

The watch meant too much to him for him to leave it be-hind. It had cost men their lives and he was not prepared to forget it easily.* He grinned as he found it, tucking the chain

* See Jubal Cade – *The Hungry Gun*.

55

through the buttonholes of his vest as he dropped the big hunter into a pocket.

'A watch?' Canfield's voice was shocked and angry. 'A fucking watch?'

'Language, Reverend,' Jubal admonished. 'What would your parishioners think?'

'Keep your mouth shut and follow me,' grated Canfield. 'If Tyree hadn't sent you, I'd let you rot here.'

The voice contained the same resonant tones Jubal had heard in the mission building, but now they were harsher, more urgent. They implied a degree of desperate purpose that was further supported by the pocket-model Navy Colt the minister held firmly in his big right hand. He closed his mouth and followed Canfield out on to the sidewalk. Around the corner of the jail, hidden in the shadows of an alley, stood a pony and a covered trap. Canfield ushered Jubal into the vehicle and climbed alongside, whipping the animal into a fast trot away from the marshal's office.

They rode in silence, turning right and then right again until they came back on to mainstreet. Canfield drove the horse up the street, then pulled it off up the Alamo Road to the mission building.

'All right,' he grunted, 'get inside fast, and keep out of sight.'

Jubal obeyed, swinging down from the trap and moving swiftly over to the mission. Albuquerque boasted kerosene-fuelled street lamps along its main thoroughfare and a few of the more important secondary streets, but the Alamo Road was in a quieter part of town, mostly occupied by storehouses and commercial premises; there were no lamps around to pick out his movements. He found the door of the church latched, but unlocked, and slipped quickly inside.

The building was as dark as the surrounding streets and Jubal's hand stayed close to the Colt under his jacket as he moved past the deserted benches. He walked silently up the aisle until he reached the big pulpit and then settled down on the steps leading up to the carved eagle to wait.

Whatever it might be, the next move was up to Canfield.

Fortunately for his nerves, he did not have to wait long. A door somewhere at the back of the church closed with a soft thud and the yellow gleam of a hand-held lantern threw erratic shadows off the walls as a big figure moved towards him.

'Don't worry.' Jubal recognized Canfield's voice, less urgent now but still irritated. 'It's me, Canfield.'

Jubal let the Colt slide gently back into the holster as the preacher set the lantern down on a bench.

'Why?' he asked softly. 'Thanks for breaking me out, but why?'

'Why the hell do you think?'

The lantern's flame illuminated the patrician lines of Canfield's face, throwing the rugged contours into stark outline beneath the halo of his flowing mane of hair. But Jubal's attention was held by the man's eyes. They blazed with a cold intensity, emphasized by the flickering light, that seemed to burn deep into Jubal's mind; it was as though the man was trying to read his thoughts.

'I guess you're the man Tyree wanted me to locate.' Jubal was thinking fast, playing it by ear. 'But why didn't you say earlier?'

'Dammit to hell, Cade, do you want me to advertise what I'm doing here?' The preacher was trying hard to control his temper.

'No, I guess not.' Jubal had only a vague idea of what they were talking about, but it seemed like the right thing to say. 'It would make things difficult.'

'Damn' right.' Canfield's vocabulary had changed to suit his new role as a jailbreaker. 'The last damn' thing I want is a redneck Yankee lawman breathing down my collar.'

He paused, pulling at the stiff circle of white ringing his neck, almost as though he felt rope there.

'I took one helluva chance getting you out of jail. I hope you're worth it. Where's the message?'

'I got two,' said Jubal evenly, trying to buy time and information. 'One is that Beauregard won't get his guns or the cattle.' He waited until Canfield had finished swearing. 'The second is in a sealed package back in my room.'

57

Canfield cursed some more.

'So now we have to go back to mainstreet to get it. That's just dandy, Cade. How long d'you think Brandstat's going to stay unconscious?'

'Professionally,' grinned Jubal, 'I'd count on him waking up about now.'

'Yeah.' Canfield stood up and began to pace the floor like some restless cat, his big hands toying with the Navy Colt. 'That means I have to get it right now, before they search your things.'

Jubal wondered how long he would remain important to Canfield once the message was delivered, and what the man's attitude would be when he had the package. Jubal had seen enough of his hidden side to realize he was far removed from the benign preacher accepting invitations to tea, and he suspected a streak of pure ruthlessness. That meant his best chance of staying alive and getting safe out of town lay in holding on to the message.

'No.' His voice was quiet, but firm. 'It means I get it.'

'You'll get it, Cade. Don't doubt that.' Canfield spun around as he said it, moving with a gun-fighter's speed. 'You'll get it in the head.'

The Navy Colt was cocked and pointing between Jubal's eyes as Canfield spoke. There was no chance of beating him to the draw, and anyway Jubal needed the man to facilitate his escape.

'All right,' his voice was pitched low and even, 'I'll make a deal. I fetch you the message in return for a ride out of town. Otherwise forget it.' He grinned at the black hole threatening his life, looking past it to the furious eyes of Logan Canfield. 'You kill me now and you're a two-time loser. With me dead, the message is gone. And how will you explain a corpse – especially mine – in your church?'

'Damn you, Cade,' snarled the big man, 'whose side are you on?'

'Mine.' Jubal's voice was calm. 'Whose are you on?'

Canfield's confusion was genuine. He was very obviously taken aback by Jubal's question, as though there had never been any doubt about the matter, as though he had assumed all along they were working together.

'You don't know?'

'No.' There was no longer any reason to pretend. 'I made a promise to a dying man, that was all.'

Canfield shook his head in bewilderment, the Colt dropping down to point at the floor.

'So you're not one of us.' His voice registered surprise and a fresh upsurge of anger.

'I guess not.'

As he spoke, Jubal reached for the Colt in his shoulder holster. Canfield's gun was still pointed down and his amazement rendered his vigilance lax: it seemed a good moment to turn the tables. Jubal seized the advantage with a clean draw that would have pleased his tutor in the lethal art of hand-weaponry. Before Canfield was able to gather his senses and raise the pocket pistol, Jubal's gun was aimed at his chest, trigger slack taken up so that only the thumb holding back the hammer prevented the ·30 calibre slug from completing its deadly journey.

'We better talk fast,' Jubal said, 'after you've put the gun down.'

He waited until the weapon was on the floor, then kicked it far off to one side. Motioning Canfield to sit down, he ordered the man to talk.

'All right,' the preacher was reluctant, but recognized that he had little choice, 'but if you want to get away from this town you have to trust me. The church is a front for the operation. Tyree, me and Beauregard are in it together. Tyree brings cattle and guns up from the south to me here. I clear them through to Beauregard. He's got a set-up in Oregon, way out in the Cascades. You ever been up that way?'

Jubal shook his head.

'It's some of the roughest country I've ever seen. A man could hide away up there for ever and no one'd find him. Like Beauregard's doing.'

He broke off as a sound Jubal had heard twice before introduced a new element of menace to the darkened church.

Coming out of the shadows like a rumble of distant thunder was the deep-throated growl of a dog. Then the growl turned into a snarl that was drowned by Canfield's scream.

A big black shape launched itself from the darkness, the lantern showing up a mouth full of yellow teeth that fastened on Canfield's throat. Instinctively, Jubal swung his gun to bear down on the dog, but a heavy blow smashed his forearm to one side and the bullet blasted uselessly into the steps of the pulpit. Then something very hard hit him across the neck, rolling him off the bench on to his knees. He was trying to get up when a second blow drove him to the ground and a cold, metal cylinder pressed against his back.

'Now you jest stay right there,' grunted Ahab, 'an' let ole Strife finish the bastard off.'

From his prone position Jubal could only just see what was happening. He did not, however, need to see it clearly. Canfield's screams told the whole story in graphic vocal detail, his high-pitched yells choking off to liquid gurgles as his clutching hands fell away from Strife's head and the mastiff stood, worrying at his throat, until all sound died.

'Don't let it trouble you none,' Ahab's voice was almost conversational, 'his kind ain't worth it. An' there ain't nothin' personal in this.'

Jubal felt the rifle lift from his back, then heard a swift rush of air as it came down again. He felt the muzzle connect with his skull, ramming his face hard against the planking, then coloured lights danced across his vision and he fell into blackness.

He came to with the taste of blood in his mouth and the lantern throwing a pale light across the crumpled form of Logan Canfield. Jubal picked up his gun and crawled over to the preacher. Ahab and Strife were gone, though the bloody marks of their presence remained behind them. Canfield's throat and hands were crimson rags of tattered flesh, the bones of his hands crushed and broken, his windpipe severed so that his fast-failing heart pumped an intermittent column of blood through the gap.

Incredibly, he was still alive; just as Tyree had clung to

existence, so Canfield refused to yield. It was as though, Jubal thought, they had to pass on their mission, for Canfield was trying hard to speak. It was impossible for him to form words through the ragged wound in his throat, but somehow he forced partly coherent sounds out between gobbets of blood.

Jubal heard him say 'Beauregard' then something about the Cascades and the package and escape. He mumbled about a man called Sillers and money. Then he died.

Jubal's course of action was pretty clear, defined for him by the events of the night and by now most likely out of his control. Albuquerque was no small border town from which he could shoot his way out; nor could he slip away in the night: he wanted the money he had hidden back in his room. That meant that he had to evade capture by the marshal, who must by now be conscious again, and find a way out of the place. The first thing, whatever the odds, was to get the money – and the mysterious package – from the hotel.

He left Canfield sprawled in a pool of spreading blood that would surely provide a shock for his parishioners come the next time for service and headed for the rear door.

It opened on to an unlit alley flanked on both sides by silent buildings rising high enough to exclude what faint moonlight was trying to filter through the cloud cover. Jubal took advantage of the darkness as he slipped out of the Alamo Road mission and, hugging the shadows, began to walk back in the direction of mainstreet. It appeared no more active than usual and he crossed it quickly, dodging between the riders still parading the street despite the late hour, to duck into another alley that seemed to lead down towards the river.

Relying upon memory, he turned left around a warehouse and headed up a muddy, stinking lane in what he hoped was the direction of the hotel.

Twice, he had to step over the supine bodies of drunks, sleeping off their load of alcohol in the doorways of the dark-shrouded buildings that hid the lane in a cloak of blackness. He saw no one else, and after a while the buildings on one side gave way to high-standing wood fencing and the pungent odour of penned horses. Jubal could hear the animals moving restlessly in the night and, just, make out their shifting bodies in the pale moonlight.

He was, he realized, moving alongside the stockyards that faced the rear of Harve Johnson's hotel.

He shifted his position to the other side of the alley, looking up to study the back wall of the rooming house. His room was on the second floor of the building, its window two down from the corner and unlit. That meant that either Marshal Brandstat had not yet got around to checking the room or was, maybe, inside waiting. Jubal decided on taking a chance and choosing to believe the room was still clear; anyway, he needed the money and the rifle inside.

The hotel was backed by a covered walk, cluttered with garbage cans and used-up furniture, but the shingled roof of the porchway looked secure enough to take his weight.

He moved over to the rear door and pressed his ear against the frame. The hotel was quiet so he hauled a dilapidated chair to the edge of the boardwalk and, gingerly, stepped up on to the seat. It gave him the height he needed to top the edge of the porch roof and drag himself up. Carefully, taking pains to make no noise, he wriggled up the slanting surface until his face was level with the window ledge. The room was dark and quiet, and as far as Jubal could see there was no one on the inside.

Warily, he climbed to his feet, grasping the frame on either side. Then, holding on with one hand, he pried at the bottom of the window. It was open and loose and it moved up with a surprising lack of noise.

Jubal swung inside with a fast, cat-silent movement that left him crouched, Colt in his hand, on the faded carpet. He holstered the gun when he was sure the room was empty of waiting lawmen and lifted the mattress. The oilskin packets remained where he had left them and after reaching behind the closet, he stuffed them into his saddlebag. The room had not been searched and there was no noise outside to indicate imminent danger. None the less, Jubal felt it expedient to get away from the hotel as swiftly as possible, so he hefted the saddlebags on to his left shoulder, grabbed the Spencer in his right hand, and opened the door. The corridor was empty and dark, but he could hear the sound of someone moving around downstairs. He paced back to the window and threw the saddlebags into the alley, then, holding the rifle, he climbed back to the ground.

His arrival and departure went unseen in the dark Sunday night.

As he moved away from Johnson's hotel he saw a sudden blaze of light from the window he had just vacated. Swiftly, he flattened himself against the wall, watching the spread of illumination across the alley as someone hung a lantern from the window.

'He's been here, that's for sure.' Jubal recognized Brandstat's voice.

'Yeah, but where the hell is he now?' It was a deputy speaking, his enquiry answered by Harve Johnson.

'He can't be far. I checked the room about twenty minutes ago an' it was clean. The rifle was still here an' the window was closed.'

'OK.' Brandstat sounded like he had a sore head and wanted to find the man who had given it to him. 'I want a search party. We're gonna comb every damn' backstreet in this town until we find him. Tommy, you go watch Levy's stable. His horse is there an' that greedy bastard'll sell it back to him if he shows up. Make sure he don't ride out.'

Jubal heard Tommy leave the room as the marshal began to speak again.

'Vince, you take Charley an' some others. Stake out the riverfront. Jim-boy, you start lookin' in the saloons. I'll get to work on the streets. If we ain't found him by sun-up, we'll meet back at the jail.'

Jubal wondered how he was going to get out of town and studied the corral across the way speculatively. His thoughts of stealing a horse were abruptly curtailed by the sound of bootheels on the shingled roof over his head and the sudden appearance of denim-trousered legs directly in front of him. The legs slid off the roof as the deputy dropped to the ground, cursing as he landed in the mud.

He cursed again as he saw Jubal, but the oath was cut short by the barrel of Jubal's rifle. It swung around in a short arc that ended along the man's left temple, dropping him silently to the ground.

Jubal didn't wait for the repercussions. Instead, he took off at a run up the alley, ignoring the shouts echoing behind him. He needed cover fast. And after that, a way out of Albuquerque.

The lane's clinging mud slowed him, but he ran as fast as he could manage, trying hard to put distance between himself and Kile Brandstat. Twice shots rang off the woodwork to his side, followed by shouts from his pursuers and the people sleeping inside the darkened buildings. Then he ducked around a corner, moving in the direction of mainstreet. The stockyards followed the curve of the alley and within the fenced area the unbroken horses were shifting restlessly, spooking at the thunder of the gunfire. Jubal paused long enough to trigger three shots back down the lane, aiming high to put them over the heads of Brandstat's men. Then he powered himself fast across the alley, rolling as he hit the fence so that he came up on his feet in amongst the horses. He set his shoulder against the gate rail, pushing up and out, straining at the heavy poles. The gate shifted under the pressure, lifting out of the simple iron bracket holding it shut. Jubal ignored the buffeting of the shifting horses, hoping they would avoid his feet as they stamped around him. He could smell their fear-sweat and hear the harsh snorting as they blew air through nervous nostrils. Then the gate was open and the horses going through.

Pushed on by Jubal's yells, they exploded into the narrow alley like a bad dream coming true. Pintos and bays jostled for position as they raced, shoulder to shoulder, straight at Brandstat's men. A big grey with rolling, crazy eyes knocked Jubal hard back against the fence, then paused long enough to kick a deputy slower than the others in finding cover clean across the alley. Jubal heard the man scream as the unshod rear hooves rammed into his stomach, pitching the lantern he held high in the air so that it fell and shattered, spreading a pool of flaming kerosene around the hooves of the following horses. Totally maddened now, the ponies ran stone-blind through the flames, seeking escape. Brandstat's men were scattered, dodging into doorways, climbing fences and porchfronts as they tried to avoid the stampede.

Jubal took full advantage of the confusion. Screened by the crazed animals, he headed out of the corral towards mainstreet. He didn't know if more lawmen were waiting for him there, but he didn't have any other place to go. So he trusted to luck and his gun and moved forwards.

The far end of the alley grew suddenly dark, something blocking out the streetlamps and lantern flames. Jubal checked his rush, angling the Spencer to level on the wagon that had appeared across the exit. It was a four-wheel flatbed, with a rise of grubby canvas curving head-high over the base. Something was painted on to the faded white of the covering, but Jubal was unable to make out the words in the darkness. He could hear, though, and the message was unmistakable.

'Guess you must be Cade.' The voice was deep, rich and resonant, like Canfield's. 'Get inside fast, afore you're spotted.'

With no alternative hiding place, Jubal chose to take a chance. He ran on up the alley, coming alongside the wagon as it moved slowly past the narrow street. The canvas was lifted from the inside and he hefted his saddlebags over the wooden sideflap as he grabbed at a handhold. He was carried along for a couple of paces, then got a knee over the edge and rolled into the dark interior.

'Why, *mister*!' giggled a feminine voice, 'if you want to wrestle you might introduce yourself first.'

'Sorry, ma'am,' murmured Jubal as he rolled off the woman who had lifted the canvas. 'I wasn't expecting so soft a landing.'

Her giggles were cut short by a peremptory demand from the driver.

'Get him hidden, Vicky, and get yourself up here. Fast.'

Before Jubal could protest, or ask what was going on, the woman was piling blankets over him and pulling crates around and over the blankets. Through their cover, Jubal could faintly hear the driver speaking again.

'It's not perfect, but it's the best we can do. Stay right there and don't make a sound.'

Jubal doubted that he could be heard at all, so he stretched out on the bed of the wagon, his head pillowed on the saddle-bags and the Spencer held ready to use close beside him. He could feel the wagon moving slowly up mainstreet towards the edge of town and after a while, he shifted around so that his face was pressed against the side of the vehicle. Through a crack in the planking, he could make out the dark shapes of the buildings, illuminated by the torches and lanterns carried by Brandstat's men. Once the wagon stopped and Jubal listened to the driver arguing with a deputy; he must have won, because they began to move again soon after.

Then, when he was beginning to feel claustrophobic beneath the concealing blankets, Jubal felt the wagon stop again.

'All right, Cade.' It was the driver. 'You can come out now.'

Gratefully, Jubal pushed the boxes and blankets to one side and rose to his feet. The inside of the thing was high enough for him to stand up, the tall metal hoops supporting the canvas festooned with an array of bottles, shelves and cupboards lashed to a wooden framework. The floor of the wagon was cluttered with packing cases, wooden kegs and the parapher-nalia of a travelling medicine show. Gaudily painted strips of tarpaulin were thrown in untidy bundles amongst folding chairs and collapsible tables, down the centre lay a bedroll and beside it, looking incredibly unlikely, was a small harmonium. Jubal pushed his way through the litter to he tailboard and jumped to the ground, holding the Spencer.

'No need for that.' The speaker was a tall man who looked as though he might have Indian blood from the handsome, aquiline set of his face, marred only by a slackness around his mouth. He was dressed in an impeccable suit of pale grey broadcloth, the jacket held wide to show he carried no gun. 'I'm not armed and we're near enough friends anyway.'

'I don't know you, mister.' Jubal held the Spencer ready on the man's chest. 'I'm grateful for your help, but I'd like to know why.'

66

'Indeed, I can understand that,' smiled the driver, 'so permit me to introduce myself properly. My name is Sillers. Royston Sillers, at your service.'

'Sillers?' Jubal had heard the name somewhere before. Abruptly, he remembered where: Canfield had said it just before he died.

'Indeed.' Sillers' smile was all gleaming teeth, offset by a head of wavy iron-grey hair that, allied to his lazy, cultured voice, lent an air of solid respectability to his demeanour. Under other circumstances, Jubal might easily have taken the man for a prosperous banker or businessman; as things stood, he was unsure what Sillers might be.

'You've heard the name? Good. It makes things easier. I suppose poor Logan mentioned me.'

'Canfield? Yeah, he did.' Jubal wondered where Sillers figured in the mystery surrounding the dead preacher. He could be part of the gun-running operation, or just a messenger; Jubal wasn't sure. He started to speak, but Sillers cut him short.

'Logan and I were working together. He asked me to collect a message you brought him. That was before his unfortunate demise.' He paused delicately. 'I suppose you are innocent of his murder? I heard Brandstat was hunting you, so I came looking. It was just as well that I did, in the circumstances.'

'I can't argue with that,' grinned Jubal, lowering the rifle, 'and don't worry: I didn't kill Canfield. That was a man called Ahab.'

'Ahab!' Sillers was genuinely alarmed. 'I heard he was around, but I never saw him, thank God. Where is he now?'

'Last time I saw him,' Jubal replied, 'was in the church, just before he hit me.'

Sillers seemed relieved, a degree of tension shrugging from his elegant shoulders as he beckoned Jubal over to the fire the woman was starting. As tall as Jubal, she was surprisingly attractive, her blonde curls partially hidden beneath a black shawl. She smiled as he squatted down by the fire, indicating the cooking pots standing ready for use.

'You must be hungry. I'll have food ready in a while.'

'I'm grateful, ma'am,' grinned Jubal, exposing his broken front teeth in a boyish grin that belied the tension he felt.

Sillers must have sensed Jubal's unease, for he produced a bottle of whiskey and poured two measures before hauling three chairs from the wagon. He unfolded the canvas-hung structures and set them around the fire, then extracted a table of similar design on which he set the whiskey bottle. Jubal seated himself, leaning the Spencer against the chair, and listened. All around them, the prairie was silent except for the occasional scuffling of some small animal; overhead the sky stretched wide and clear like a deep blue canopy pricked with light. It was warm and the quiet of the lazy night produced a strange feeling of comfort as the unlikely trio sat around the fire.

'I should explain,' began Sillers, 'that Vicky and I earn a modest living purveying medicine.' He indicated the wagon and in the moonlight, Jubal could read the words painted there: 'Doctor Royston Sillers and his Travelling Medicine Show.' He grinned; so Sillers was a travelling quack, selling coloured water to cowboys too ignorant to know what they were drinking. Sillers saw the grin and shrugged.

'An ignoble profession, perhaps, but one that allows me to travel without undue hindrance. As you may have noticed, I can come and go much as I please.'

Remembering his getaway from Albuquerque, Jubal could not argue.

'So,' Sillers went on, 'I serve as a messenger between Canfield and Beauregard and my immediate concern is with the message you carry. Believe me, Cade, it's vitally important. Beauregard must get it.'

'Just who is Beauregard?' Jubal asked, wondering why the message could not be entrusted to the interstate mail relays.

'You don't know?' Sillers, like Canfield had been, was genuinely shocked by Jubal's ignorance. 'But surely, you're one of us?'

Jubal shook his head, watching the quack's mouth gape in surprise. 'No. So tell me who *you* are.'

Sillers stood up, holding his glass, and paced slowly to the

68

far side of the fire. He looked at Jubal for a long time without speaking, his handsome face illuminated by the flames.

He took a long swallow and opened his mouth to speak. Then, far away, Jubal heard a heavy cough. Sillers dropped his glass and stepped backwards, his hands dangling limp by his side as his face went slack. His knees buckled and he folded slowly to the ground, as though praying. He didn't say anything, just toppled forwards into the puddle of blood spraying from the hole in the centre of his forehead.

He was dead before he hit the ground, the bullet that drilled the hole in his face exiting through the back of his skull so that most of his rear cranium was blown away.

Vicky began to scream as Jubal grabbed the Spencer and found cover behind the wagon. The ·30 calibre rifle was no match for the gun that had killed Sillers, but Jubal's instinct was for immediate defence. He knew there was only one kind of gun that could kill so devastatingly at that kind of range: a ·50 calibre Sharps buffalo rifle; the kind Ahab carried. Far off he heard a deep-throated baying, then the night fell silent again.

Jubal walked over to the corpse and studied the damage.

'Dammit,' he muttered, absently picking up Sillers' glass and throwing it off to one side, 'every time someone decides to uncork themselves, there's someone else to put the stopper in.'

# CHAPTER SEVEN

The woman stopped screaming when Jubal slapped her hard across the face, subsiding into a muffled sobbing that was partially consoled by the whiskey he thrust into her hand. Gradually, she regained control, enough, at least, to attempt to answer the questions Jubal threw at her.

Her name was Victoria Kennedy and she was twenty-three years old, the daughter of an immigrant Irish couple who had staked a claim to a dust-dry packet of Texas sand along the Brazos river. When Kiowas hit the soddy four months after Patrick Kennedy had finished building it, his daughter had seen him die with a lance stuck through his belly. He had taken a long time going, but not so long as his wife. Twelve Kiowa bucks had taken their pleasure of Bridget Kennedy before their war chief slit her throat. The delay afforded by the multiple rape had saved Victoria's life: the Indians were sated for the time being, so they slung her across a mustang and took her with them. That night, before the bucks got around to laying the girl in the circle, the Texas Rangers who had been tailing the raiding party for the last four days caught up. Texican justice was short, sharp and untempered with any kind of mercy. Nine warriors died in the first volley, one was ridden down in the charge and trampled to death by a whooping Ranger, and the sole survivor was left in the sand, hands and feet tied together with strips of wet rawhide that were looped around his throat. One of the Rangers explained to the weeping sixteen-year old that the rawhide would dry in the morning sun and choke the buck to death. She stopped crying then.

The Rangers had taken her to their station in Waco, where she had three choices if she wanted to eat. She could serve table in one of the local eating houses; busk drinks as a saloon girl; or enter a cat house. She tried the first choice for six months before the explicit attentions of the diners persuaded her that the cat house offered a greater degree of security, a whole lot more money and more comfort than she was used to.

Then Royston Sillers turned up. Good-looking, well-mannered and throwing money around like it was Confederate bills. It took him exactly two days to talk her into joining his enterprise, forty-two of those hours being spent in bed. That had been six years before.

'There was three of us then,' she said tearfully, 'Roy had an old-timer with him, a man called Rogers. He always wore real fancy shirts, an' he sang real nice. Used to bring in the customers with his singin' an' his fancy pony tricks. He could even make his horse dance. Then he met a real pretty girl called Dale an' quit us to get married. Now I'm on my own again.'

She burst into fresh tears and threw her arms around Jubal. For a moment he felt longings he had not experienced since Mary's death: the girl was very close and her hair smelled fragrant as it brushed his face. But then he pushed the moment aside and began to ask her about Sillers.

She couldn't tell him very much and it was soon obvious that the travelling quack had kept his clandestine ventures to himself. Jubal learned that the medicine show had travelled the length of America, moving mostly around the southern states, but every so often driving far north to Montana and Oregon and North Dakota. Up there, Sillers had largely forgotten his pseudo-doctoring, concentrating instead on meeting people who usually arrived at night and left before the sun came up. They seemed, said Victoria, to be military gentlemen, always very correct and secretive in their dealings. Like any good hooker, she had asked no questions and refused to see anything that Sillers didn't want her to see.

But she remembered the road they had taken and the town called Deliverance that was the road show's favourite stopping place.

Jubal kept feeding her whiskey as she talked, and when she finally sank slowly to the ground, he hauled the bedroll out of

71

the wagon and wrapped her in blankets, stroking her blonde hair until she drifted off into tipsy slumber.

Then he went through the wagon.

For a quack, Royston Sillers had maintained a surprising arsenal of weapons. Hung on thongs behind the drapes that covered the wagon's canvas topping were Civil War Spencers, lever-action Winchesters, three ·52 calibre Sharps carbines and a selection of handguns that ranged from the ubiquitous Colt Peacemaker to single-action Remington revolvers imported from England. The kegs he had previously thought to contain patent cures held as many cartridges as they did sure-fire, quick-death medicines.

When he had finished checking through Sillers' strange cargo, Jubal went to his own saddlebags. They were still under the blankets that had hidden him and they still held the two oilskin envelopes.

He pushed the one with the money to the bottom of the bag, yanked a long-bladed knife from the carving block that lay on the floor of the wagon, and cut through the wax seals. His fingers found a wad of paper and he pulled the lantern closer as he began to read.

The first few sheets were maps, hand-written and hard to decipher, their inscriptions abbreviated into some kind of personal shorthand. They showed, to judge from the shadings, a mountainous area and Jubal felt it safe to assume the large C lettered in the centre stood for Cascades. Further capitals seemed to represent towns and there were broken lines that could have indicated trails or railroads; most probably trails, thought Jubal, for even though his knowledge of the geography of North-west America was, at best, sketchy, he was fairly sure there were no rail lines yet put down. One sheet put the close-detail maps into better perspective. It was a political map showing the boundaries between Washington, Oregon, Idaho and Nevada, with contour lines indicating the razor-back ridges that held the northern states in a stony fist. If the maps were reliable, Sillers had been heading for some of the roughest territory in the United States.

Another sheet looked like a quartermaster's supply list.

Quantities of weapons, ranging from hand-guns to rifles, were carefully marked down, together with lists of provisions, medical supplies and clothing. Against each quantity someone had put a tick in indelible pencil and a flourishing signature at the bottom of the list looked to decipher as 'Tyree'.

Then Jubal found a sealed envelope, addressed to Beauregard. He broke the seals and began to read.

Several minutes later he knew where Tyree and the wagons had been heading, and the purpose of their journey. If the Apaches had not put so abrupt an end to his journey, Tyree would have delivered seven hundred head of beef cattle and enough weaponry to kit out a small army to Mordecai Beauregard in Washington State. Canfield was to have acted as middleman, introducing Tyree to Sillers, who was to act as guide to Beauregard's headquarters in the Cascades.

Jubal was no wiser as to the purpose of Beauregard's venture; but he intended to learn more.

He had the maps and the woman to guide him to the meeting place, Sillers' wagon for transport and seven weeks to make the rendezvous. If he missed the date specified in the papers, Beauregard would disappear back into the mountains for a month. He was, it seemed obvious, hiding from something: Jubal was sufficiently curious to want to know why.

He drained his glass and settled down to sleep, letting the pieces of the human jigsaw run through his mind. They were beginning to fit together, only Ahab refused to fall into place with his hunt for the white-haired man and his murderous attacks on Canfield and Sillers. He was the wild card in the deck and Jubal would have to wait for him to appear again before he could be woven into the pattern. Jubal went to sleep thinking about the one-legged man and his ugly dog.

Dawn broke the way prairie mornings were meant to, the sun appearing dramatically over the rim of the flatlands, the long, black shadows of the giant cactus plants chasing the last grey remnants of night into yellow-white, heat-hazed oblivion.

Vicky was already awake, kneeling by the fire as she turned bacon in the pan. She smiled as Jubal pushed his blanket aside and carried a mug of coffee over.

73

'It's black and strong,' she grinned, 'but we've got sugar and cans of milk.'

'Black and strong sounds good, thanks,' Jubal answered her grin, accepting the steaming mug.

He drank the coffee where he sat, then washed and shaved in the water she brought him. Victoria Kennedy was obviously the kind of woman who accepted a subservient role, and Jubal seemed to have replaced Sillers – if only temporarily – as captain of her particular ship.

When he had finished he hunkered down by the fire and took the plate of bacon she offered. Canned tomatoes were brought from the wagon, accompanied by thick slabs of white bread and more coffee. The wagon and the woman would slow him down on the long journey northwards, but they looked like providing ample compensation in the way of creature comforts.

He hitched the horse up as Victoria scoured the plates, then scattered the fire and climbed on to the wagon. Ahead of them lay the better part of one thousand miles of mountains and desert country: Jubal doubted he could make the rendezvous in time.

# CHAPTER EIGHT

'You'll never make it.'

The woman's voice was flat and drawn with the tired accents of finality. She pushed a strand of sweat-soaked blonde hair from her eyes and stared blindly into the heat haze.

'Never's a big word,' grunted Jubal, wishing that the tongue he passed over his lips had enough saliva on it to wet them. They were beginning to crack in the heat. 'We'll make it.'

He wished he was as confident as he sounded, but Deliverance seemed an awful long way away and the horse was very tired, nearly as exhausted as the two people it was hauling slowly northwards.

The wagon was a tiny speck of moving darkness crawling painfully across the burning white of the Great Salt Lake. The last waterhole they had seen was four days behind them, and their butt had run dry around noon of the previous day. Jubal had elected to head straight for his destination, rather than follow the easier route skirting the Rockies' eastern flank. The going had been hard as they pushed along the narrow mountain trails across Colorado and Utah, heading by way of Mesa Verde for the Green River. More than once, he had paced ahead of the wagon, lighting the trail with a hand-held lantern as the woman urged the nervous horse over the rocks. They had lost the better part of a day south of Spanish Fork, when the wagon hit a sink hole and settled axle-deep in the clinging mud. Jubal had to chop brush and wade into the mire to settle a solid carpet beneath the wheels before they could haul the vehicle free.

Then, as summer was fading into fall, they reached the Great Salt Lake.

It was the breaking point for Victoria Kennedy. She stared apprehensively at the vast expanse of dazzling bleached-bone whiteness stretching out before them and burst into tears. Jubal had muttered something reassuring and urged the horse forwards. Now he was wondering if they should have skirted the desert.

The horse made up his mind for him: it snickered softly and collapsed in the traces. Jubal was too tired to curse, so he simply climbed down and walked around to the gaunt animal. One glance told him it was finished; the outline of its rib-cage was sticking through its salt-caked hide and its breathing was a frothy wheeze. Jubal listened for a moment to the asthmatic sound, then drew the Colt. He placed the muzzle against the pony's skull and pulled the trigger. Death was immediate, a whole lot quicker, thought Jubal, than his would be in this god-forsaken wilderness.

Behind him, the woman began to cry again.

'Now what?' She wailed. 'We're dead for sure without the horse.'

'Ma'am,' grunted Jubal, 'there was a man I knew once down around Illinois, had a saying for everything. Guess that right now he'd tell you where there's life there's hope. Me, I just hope we can stay alive long enough to find water, but it's not about to come looking for us. So let's start walking.'

Faced with no alternative other than dying where she sat, Victoria climbed into the rear of the wagon and began to bundle supplies into a patchwork valise. Somehow, the stark reality of the situation had shaken her free of the numb despair that had gripped her and she approached the task with brusque efficiency. Jubal watched her as he gathered the stuff he wanted. There was little enough: his rifle and several boxes of spare cartridges; the medical bag; an empty canteen; and the papers and money he was carrying. Then, two lonely figures in a sun-baked emptiness, they began to trudge over the salt flats.

The heat was unbelievable. It hit them like the devil's breath, burning down into their lungs, transforming their clothes into sweat-sodden, itchy rags. Jubal could feel it through the soles of his boots just as he could feel the salt drying and caking in his hair. Speech was impossible: it was simply too much effort, and they needed every ounce of waning energy to push one foot out in front of the other.

The night brought no succour. The heat evaporated from

the flats like a flame going out in a wind, and the cold set in. There was no brush for a fire, so they were forced to huddle close together, trying hard to ignore the irritation of salty skin rubbing on rough cloth, in a desperate attempt to stay warm. Sex played no part in their intimacy, it was as far from their exhausted thoughts as the idea of water was close.

Finally, it was sheer exhaustion that made them sleep.

And the sun that woke them.

It hit Jubal's face like a blow, waking him as abruptly as would a flame touched to his skin. He sat up, blinking in the glare, and pulled the woman to her feet. Reluctantly, she stood, rubbing at the salt coating her eyelids. She was far removed from the pretty girl Jubal had seen back near Albuquerque. Her hair was a matted thatch of dirty blonde, her face salt-white and thin, blisters were rising on her lips and there was a look of pure resignation in her eyes.

Without speaking, she began to walk.

They moved like automatons, forcing themselves onwards against the protests of their aching limbs, only the soul-deep instinct for survival persuading their bodies to keep moving. As the sun climbed towards its highest point, Jubal called a halt. Beside him, Victoria collapsed in a crumpled bundle of stained petticoats as he marvelled at the amount of clothing a woman could carry.

His mouth was so dry now that it hurt him to speak, but he forced words thickly through his lips.

'We'll get a whole lot farther if you shed some skirts.'

He found it impossible to say any more and gestured instead at the voluminous folds of her underclothing.

She nodded dumbly and began to unbutton her blouse. Jubal could barely see her, close though she was, through the sweat clouding his vision, but with a typically feminine gesture she motioned him to turn around. When she touched his shoulder he turned to find several frilly garments spread over the salt. Dark stockings lay beside a whalebone corset that must have been agony to wear in the heat, and, close by, the black skirt she had worn. Victoria sat, dressed now in a loose chemise, a cotton petticoat draped around her shoulders and a

77

rueful smile on her lips.

'I guess,' she said throatily, 'that enough men seen me naked for this to make no difference.'

Jubal did his best to look cheerful.

'Ma'am,' he doffed the grey derby as he spoke, 'you look pretty as a picture.'

'Yeah,' she didn't sound as though she believed him, 'and like that friend of yours might have said: you come into the world naked, so you might as well go out the same way.'

Jubal didn't reply, instead he gathered her discarded underclothes together and began to rip the filmy material apart. By the time he was finished they had a serviceable tent that might offer a little protection against the sun, and a foot-wide circle of torn silk.

They waited out the noonday heat beneath the sheathing of petticoats and then began to walk again.

As night fell, they pushed on until the woman complained of the cold. Jubal would have preferred to keep moving, but accepted, through sheer necessity, the need to let her rest. He draped his jacket over her shoulders and then staggered a few paces away. He scooped a shallow hollow in the ground and set his hat in the indentation. He pulled the circle of silk from his trouser pocket and worked a hole in the centre with a dirty fingernail; then, using salt to weight the material, he settled the stuff over the derby so that it formed an inverted cone, with the hole at the lowest point, over the bowl of the hat.

It was, to say the very least, a crude water cache, but Jubal hoped that the silk would catch enough of the night's cold to condense some moisture to keep them going a little longer.

And, anyway, it was the best hope they had.

In the morning the silk was moist. There was no water in his upturned hat and barely enough on the material to wet Victoria's lips, though she sucked avidly enough.

As he pulled her to her feet and led her off across the seemingly unending salt flats, Jubal knew that he could not last another day without water. He was not sure that Victoria would succeed in keeping pace for even that length of time, and he wondered as he plodded relentlessly on what he would do if she collapsed.

He found out when she pitched face down on the salt two hours later: he picked her up and kept on walking. He even managed to keep moving for another hour before his legs gave out. He was trembling from the effort and the soul-sapping heat, mentally cursing the desert, Tyree, Canfield and anything else that came to mind, when his knees folded under him and he dropped the woman. She fell unconscious beneath him and as he dragged a length of petticoat over her exposed shoulders everything went black.

High above them, vultures circled lazily around the sky.

The black-pinioned undertakers of the desert wheeled, stark against the blue-white, in easy spirals, drifting gently down as the movement below ceased. Their far-seeing, almost preternatural senses told them a feast waited on the ground: two carcases of soft flesh ready for the taking. Beaks open in silent anticipation, they closed on their prey. Typical of their carrion breed, they landed heavily on clumsy, clawed feet, several yards from their intended victims. Hungry, but none the less willing to wait until they were sure, they spread themselves in a morbid circle round the bodies of Jubal and the woman.

Time passed without movement and gradually the birds grew bolder, lifting their heavily-taloned feet like macabre dancers drawing closer to the centre of some ritual circle.

The largest, ugliest of the things finally plucked up sufficient courage to approach within pecking range. Uttering a nervous croak, it jabbed its curved beak at Jubal's exposed hand.

When the man's limb did not respond to the attack, the vulture cawed its triumph and waddled forwards. It continued to peck anxiously at the prone forms as it climbed on to Jubal's back, sinking its talons into the yielding flesh as it sought the best purchase for its eating. It was swiftly joined by the more timid members of the carrion crew, drawing courage from their leader's example and accompanying him on his ghoulish climb.

Soon the two bodies were obscured beneath a noisy, black-winged carpet of cackling, pecking death.

Jubal remained totally oblivious to the assault upon his body, too far gone to even be conscious of the savage wounds inflicted by the viciously-curved beaks. Beneath him, Victoria was largely protected from the birds' ravages, her supine form covered by Jubal's body.

They might well have died there, leaving their bones as two more forgotten markers of the salt desert's murderous power. But instead they were saved.

The same heavy crack that had presaged the death of Sillers, magnified now by the Salt Lake's stillness, echoed out over the waste. A vulture's head exploded in a bloody miasma of stained feathers and at the sudden demise of one of their clan, the other scavengers took flight. Squawking, scrabbling, beating madly at the boiling air with their heavy wings, they flapped up from the bodies. Three failed to gain enough height as three more shots rang out, their corpses falling ungainly to the ground as a solitary figure, accompanied by a loping black dog, rode slowly out of the haze.

Ahab reached the two people and dismounted. Close by, the dog called Strife watched the birds as though he anticipated snatching one out of the sky. His master ignored him as he pushed Jubal over on to his back.

'Figgered you might need some help, pilgrim,' he chuckled, dribbling water over Jubal's lips, 'an' it looks like I brung it jest in time.'

He exposed his blackened teeth in a sardonic grin as Jubal opened his eyes and then shut them again when he saw the one-legged man leering at him.

'What's the trouble, Jubal, ole friend?' Even though Ahab was smiling he remained menacing. 'You ain't pleased to see me?'

Instead of answering, which he couldn't do anyway, Jubal grabbed at the canteen, luxuriating in the sheer life-giving pleasure of warm, brackish water. He drank deep, swilling the liquid around his parched mouth, spitting out salt and then swallowing again. He would have drunk more, had Ahab's gnarled hand not pulled the flask from his grip.

'Now that's enough, feller,' grunted the oldster, 'any more

an' you're gonna bloat up like a horse on blow weed. Take it easy whiles I attend to the woman.'

He emphasized his sentence by rolling Jubal to one side where the dog leered, panting into his face, and applying the canteen to Victoria's mouth. She lay still as water trickled over her lips, then came to and, like Jubal, grabbed for the life source.

Ahab let her drink for a while before corking the water bottle, then he hunkered down, stretching his wooden leg out before him and watching the two sun-drained wrecks lying immobile on the sand.

Blood was oozing from the beak wounds on Jubal's hands and back, and as the water performed its life-giving work, he became conscious of Strife's tongue lapping at the suppurations. Instinctively, he rolled away from the dog, eliciting a throaty growl as he pushed its mouth away.

'Careful, son,' chuckled Ahab, 'you ain't hardly in shape to argue with him.'

'Don't plan to,' Jubal replied thickly, 'unless he keeps giving me lip.'

'You're as prickly as ever, even with yore life saved by us wandering Samaritans.'

Ahab's empty blue eyes stared hard at Jubal as he spoke, though his tone was almost friendly.

'Wandering, hell.' Jubal pushed himself to a sitting position. 'You weren't wandering. The only way you could have found us was by sitting on our trail.'

'Could be.' Ahab exposed the wreckage of his scalp as he wiped sweat from the scar tissue. 'Jest be thankful I was around. Otherwise you'd be buzzard bait by now.'

'Yeah,' Jubal had to concede the point. 'Thanks for that You saved our lives. But what happens now?'

'Why, son,' giggled Ahab, 'you ain't more'n a day's ride from Ogden. I guess I'll aid you two poor pilgrims along the road aways an' then foller my own path.'

Jubal was too exhausted – and too thankful for life – to question the strange old man further, so he rested where he lay as Ahab fed more water to Victoria. When she was recovered enough to stand up, he lifted her on to his own horse and motioned for Jubal to follow him.

'You jest keep puttin' one foot afront t' other,' he grinned, 'an' I'll bring you in to Ogden.'

Jubal nodded without speaking and began to walk.

There were a whole lot of questions he wanted to ask the scalped man, but right now they could wait. Right now, he was concentrating on keeping up with his unlikely rescuer, thinking hard about the water in the old man's canteen.

Ahab doled it out carefully through the long afternoon and then, as dusk fell, he halted the pony and lifted the woman to the ground. Without speaking, he walked out over the darkening salt flats, his head tilted down as though looking for a dropped coin. He paced in widening circles until he suddenly stopped and lifted his wooden leg. With an abrupt downwards movement, he rammed the peg into the salt. Then he dropped to his knees and scooped at the bone-white stuff. Fascinated, Jubal walked over to watch him.

The oldster had dug a small hole and was watching it carefully. As Jubal peered over his shoulder, he saw dirty-looking liquid seeping up from the sub-soil.

'It's allus there if you know where to look.' Ahab sounded pleased with himself. 'Ain't ready to drink yet, but if'n we filter it a little bitty it's gonna see us through.'

He busied himself with his canteen as Jubal went back to the woman, sitting tired close to the two animals.

'Jubal,' she whispered as he seated himself beside her, 'who is he?'

'I guess you could say he's our guardian angel,' answered Jubal.

'Angel?' came the reply. 'If he's an angel I think I'll change my religion.'

# CHAPTER NINE

Ogden had two saving virtues: clean water and a branch line of the Union Pacific. The first offered Jubal a chance to wash himself free of the sweat and the salt accumulated over the past days; the second, a fast trip north into Washington. East of the city, the Union Pacific and the Central Pacific branched respectively to the north and south; Ogden sat astride a branch line linking the north-eastern edge of the Great Salt Lake to the railroad spurring along the curve of the Snake River, northwards to the Columbia, and Portland in Oregon.

The rails would save a whole lot of valuable time, carrying him closer to his goal than any horse could manage in the same span.

So he was grateful when Ahab led his two dried-out charges into the city.

It was a neat, orderly place, designed upon straight, juxtaposed lines of intersecting streets that fell away in orderly rows from the main thoroughfare. The houses were nowhere higher than three storeys, and built mostly of timber, although once in a while a brick-built structure showed itself amongst the bleached pine and peeling paint of the main mass.

Ahab led them directly to a hotel on the outskirts of town, lifting Victoria from the saddle to carry her into the vestibule. Wearily, Jubal followed, cradling his few possessions in his arms.

'Well, that's it, son,' grunted the oldster. 'I said I'd bring you outta the desert an' I did. Figger that pays you off fer savin' me back in Albuquerque.'

'I guess so,' Jubal replied, 'but it doesn't answer my questions.'

He watched Ahab grinning with some kind of malevolent glee, torn between gratitude and the urgent desire to rip answers from the one-legged man's fetid mouth.

'Why now,' Ahab said softly, 'what questions might they be?'

'Your dog killed Canfield,' said Jubal slowly, 'and then you shot Sillers. Why? And why did you bother to save us?'

Ahab chuckled, the rasping sound sending cold shivers down Jubal's spine.

'Like I told you a whole way back: I'm lookin' fer one particular man, an' I don't like folks gettin' in my way; if they do, I push them aside.'

'So why save us?' Jubal asked.

'You saved me,' said Ahab with total simplicity, 'one fer one. Now we're quits. So take warnin' that you an' me don't owe one another nuthin': you get in my way an' I'll push you aside jest like the others.'

Jubal looked into the cold blue eyes, as still as the deep-etched wrinkles on the fierce face, and nodded in agreement.

'All right. Quits from now on.'

'Good.' Ahab seemed pleased. 'I hope you don't get in the way. I'd sooner not kill you.'

'Thanks,' grinned Jubal ruefully, 'the feeling's mutual.'

Curiously, he felt a strange kinship with the old man, a kind of friendship that stemmed not from their mutual experiences, but from some fellow-feeling that lay deep-rooted in their personalities. They were, somehow, alike. And for that reason he hoped their paths would not cross in enmity.

He watched as Ahab swung his wooden leg over the saddle and whistled up the big, black dog, wondering where the old man was headed for. He waited until the stooped figure had disappeared in the haze and then turned into the hotel. It was clean and relatively cool and so he looked forward to a bath and sleep between clean sheets.

The bath came first, an hour-long, luxurious wallow in the cleanest water he'd seen in days; then sleep, the deep, rejuvenating unconsciousness that follows great physical effort. It was gloriously free of dreams or discomfort and Jubal had no idea how long it had lasted when the knocking at the door awoke him. He came off the bed, instantly alert and reaching for the Colt hidden beneath his pillow. As his bare feet hit the carpeted floor, the gun was cocked and pointing at the door. It stayed that way as he padded softly across the room.

He stood to one side of the frame, where he could fire through the opening.

'Who is it?'

'Me, Jubal. Vicky.'

'Wait.' He was moving back towards the bed as he spoke, reaching for the clothes a discreet desk clerk had had pressed for him. 'I'll be with you in just a while.'

He pulled on the trousers of the grey, English-tailored suit and quickly checked the time on the gold hunter he habitually carried in his vest pocket. It read nine o'clock and the light filtering through the drapes over the double window told him it was evening, which meant he had slept for around ten hours.

Then, still holding the gun, he opened the door.

Victoria Kennedy was standing in the doorway looking like a tousled-headed innocent. Her face was freshly washed and devoid of make-up so that, framed by her blonde curls, it afforded a picture of waif-like attractiveness at odds with her chosen profession.

She gathered her borrowed robe around her and asked if she could come in, looking at the scars that decorated Jubal's muscular chest. The grey-white tracery of knife wounds stood out against the darker skin, and Jubal grinned as he followed her gaze.

'Nothing to worry about.' His smile made him boyishly good-looking. 'I had an argument with an Indian once. He lost.'

He closed the door behind her and holstered his gun as she perched on the edge of the bed. Then he pulled on a shirt and waited for her to speak.

'What's going on?' She was composed, but nervous. 'We got you out of Albuquerque like Roy said we should, but Roy's dead now and I'm scared. Why're you so hellbent on getting to Deliverance? What's up there for you?'

'I'm not rightly sure.' Jubal chose his words carefully: he needed the woman with him, she was his only link with the mysterious Beauregard. 'But I promised someone I'd deliver a

85

message and since then people keep dying on me. I guess I want to know why.'

It was, in many ways, the best explanation he could offer. There was no real reason for him to continue his journey northwards, it would be a whole lot easier to pick up the saddlebags with Tyree's coin and his poker winnings and ride the rails eastwards to St. Louis. But some perverse obstinacy drove him to satisfy his curiosity and continue on to the Cascades.

Victoria did not share his desire.

'I don't want to know why,' she said sullenly. 'Ogden's no great shakes as towns go, but a girl could make a living here.'

'Could be,' agreed Jubal, 'but don't forget this is Mormon country. There's no great demand for your trade up here.'

'Want to bet?' snorted the woman. 'There's men here, so there's a demand. Broadcloth an' bibles don't satisfy a man where it counts.'

Jubal smiled at her pique; even whores, he thought, had their professional pride.

'Thing is, Vicky,' he switched on a smile, 'that I need you with me to point out Sillers' contacts. With the wagon gone, you're the only one who can lead me to Beauregard.'

'Tough,' she said with a finality that worried Jubal, 'but I ain't about to risk my life again. You saved me back there in the desert, an' I'm grateful, but I'm not coming any farther.'

She turned on a professional smile and moved back up the bed, resting her weight on her elbows. As she leaned back, she let the front of her robe fall away from her body, exposing firm, darkly-nippled breasts that thrust seductively forwards from her tautened upper body. She allowed her left leg to trail negligently over the side of the bed as she lifted the other to show a long, slender curve of thigh. Jubal couldn't help staring at the triangle of curly blonde hair between her legs.

She saw where he was looking and slipped the robe from her shoulders.

'I'd like to thank you for helping me, Jubal.' Her voice was a throaty, professional invitation that, for all its practised seductiveness, remained infinitely enticing. She shifted her position, so that she was stretched full-length on the bed, arms raised above her head to emphasize the full promise of her breasts, raising one knee to give Jubal a clear view of what lay between her legs. 'I'd like to thank you right now. Why don't you come here?'

Jubal stood up slowly, feeling the material of his trousers drawing tight across his groin. He had not enjoyed a woman since Mary's death and this one was, whore though she might be, very attractive indeed.

He felt sweat bead his forehead as he took an almost involuntary step towards the bed.

'Now, Jubal.' Her voice was a husky whisper that sent tremors of anticipation down his spine. 'Let me thank you now. I want you, Jubal. I want you now.'

He smiled slowly and began to unbutton his shirt, letting it slide to the floor as he moved over to the woman. Gently, he lowered himself on to the sheets, covering her body with his own. He felt her loins thrust up against him as her arms moved to encircle his neck, and looked down at her half-shut eyes and parted, red lips.

'Oh yes, Jubal,' she murmured softly, 'let me thank you.'

Jubal brought his right hand down in a short, savage blow that drove the edge of his stiffened palm hard against the side of her neck. It crashed on to the nerve cluster centred around the jugular vein, where the throat joins the shoulder. Victoria jerked as though a bullet had hit her, her head snapping back as her blue eyes clouded to a vacant glaze. She made no sound as she slumped back on to the pillows.

Jubal rolled off her body and hurried to his black medical valise. He sprung the catch and deftly extracted a small vial of colourless liquid. Then he moved to the washstand and poured a mug half-full of water. He added four drops of the liquid from the vial and stirred the mixture with his forefinger. Cradling the woman's head in the crook of his elbow, he tipped the drink down her throat, holding her jaws so that she swallowed automatically. When he had poured the entire mug into her, he let her fall back, swiftly examining her neck for serious injury. The blow would leave no damage more permanent than a slight bruising; the drug he had given her would render her unconscious for about two hours, and extremely groggy for about three more.

It took Jubal exactly forty minutes to dress, shave and find the depot of the Union Pacific. Twenty minutes later, he was back in the hotel room with two tickets for the midnight train to Portland, Oregon.

He found the keys to Victoria's room in a pocket of her robe and collected what few belongings she had brought with her. Then he spent thirty minutes buying a demure gingham dress with matching bonnet and suitable underwear, a pair of ladies' high-button shoes and a map of the north-western territory. Victoria was coming to as he returned, so he ripped up her old clothes and used the strips to bind her wrists and ankles to the bed frame. He forced a smaller quantity of the knockout drug into her mouth and went downstairs to the reception desk. There, he arranged for food to be sent up to the room, settled his bill, and purchased a bottle of whiskey.

Back in the room he sat down to the task of cleaning and checking over his guns while he contemplated his next move.

By the time he had finished, the Spencer and the Colt were in perfect, deadly order and Jubal knew exactly what he was going to do.

Ahab had gone, stopping only long enough to leave his two charges at the hotel; Jubal needed the woman with him, so he would keep her drugged long enough to get her on the train and worry about keeping her there later; his next consideration was food: he was hungry.

He folded the map he had been studying and pushed it into his saddlebag, poured a generous measure of whiskey and went to the door. Outside, a large tray rested on the faded carpet, covered with a clean, white cloth. Jubal carried it inside and examined the contents. Two thick steaks, trimmed with fried potatoes and greens, rested beside a half loaf of fresh-baked white bread, two big slabs of apple-pie formed the dessert and a pot of hot, black coffee was leaving a brown stain on the white napkin covering the base of the tray. Victoria was still oblivious, so Jubal finished both steaks, half the bread and one slice of pie, washing it all down with coffee and whiskey.

He felt better when he had finished and gathered his stuff together in preparation for leaving. Then he pulled a groggy Victoria to her feet and set about dressing her.

When she was fully clothed again, he packed the spare things he had bought into her carpetbag and checked his timepiece. There was the better part of half an hour before the train was due, so he pulled her to her feet and half-carried her down the stairs. A porter was despatched to bring down their bags and a cab summoned to the door.

Jubal tipped the porter and the cab driver well enough to earn their thanks, but not so generously that they might remember him distinctly, and waited for the train.

It came in right on time, the big light set above the cowcatcher piercing the flatlands' dark as emphatically as the howl of the whistle. Jubal stood up as the steaming, panting engine pulled past the low wooden platform, waiting until the seven cars behind had come to a halt before helping Victoria to her feet and leading her towards the nearest carriage.

'My wife is feeling unwell,' he explained to the solicitous black porter who helped lift her on board. 'If you could just show us our berth . . .'

Victoria moaned something unintelligible and Jubal put an arm carefully around her shoulders.

'There, darling. You can lie down soon. Just come this way.'

Thickly, forcing the words past the drug that slowed her limbs and clouded her mind, Victoria spoke. 'Fuck you, you damn' sneaky bastard.'

'Don't worry, darling.' Jubal couldn't help grinning. 'You'll be all right.'

He tipped the porter and closed the door of the two-berth sleeping cabin, then lifted the woman on to one of the bunks. She sank swiftly into sleep, but Jubal still took the precaution of binding her wrists and ankles. In the morning, he wanted to talk to her, about the journey and Beauregard and what he might do if she made any trouble.

She tried immediately she came to. It was mid-morning and

89

Jubal had been up and dressed for several hours, waiting for Victoria to regain consciousness.

He saw her eyes open and came across the tiny room in a single movement as her mouth opened. Before she had a chance to loose the scream building up inside her, Jubal's hand was clamped over her lips, muffling the sound so that only furious blue eyes could register her indignation. Jubal grinned pleasantly and put his mouth close to her ear.

'We'd better get a few things straight,' he said in a cold, calm voice. 'I aim to find Beauregard and you're the only person can point out his people. So I need you with me. I know you don't want to come along, but you don't have too much choice. What you *can* decide is how we do it: easy, or the hard way.'

He paused to let the words sink in.

'If you'll agree to help me find Sillers' friends, I'll make the trip there as pleasant as possible and stake you to a rail ticket back East. Make things hard for me and I'll keep feeding you Mickey Finns until we're off this train and into the mountains. Then I'll leave you to find your own way back. Think about it.'

Victoria thought about it and nodded her head. Jubal removed his hand and let her speak.

'O.K.' She seemed resigned. 'I'll go along with you. I'd like to know why Roy was killed anyway.'

'Good,' Jubal grinned, 'that makes it easier for both of us. So how about some lunch?'

She agreed eagerly and Jubal turned his back discreetly as she cleaned up, not that the ex-hooker would have cared had he watched her, but even with a woman like Victoria Jubal's natural politeness rose to the fore. So he sat on one of the pull-down seats hung from the carriage wall as water splashed in the washbasin set against the farther end of the compartment.

It was some in-built sixth sense that prompted him to turn when the splashing stopped, so that the heavy metal pitcher swinging at the side of his head glanced off his shoulder instead of his skull.

The blow numbed his left arm, but did nothing to stop the

roundhouse swing of his right. His open hand connected with Victoria's left cheek and the force of the blow hurled her sideways on to the bunk as a livid patch of red spread across her face. The pitcher fell to the floor and Jubal kicked it off to one side as he powered himself at the woman.

He pinned her down with the weight of his body, left forearm across her throat, cutting off her windpipe as his right hand grabbed her jaw. He pulled her face around so that he was staring into her eyes and it was the look on his face, rather than his words, that convinced her of her stupidity. Jubal's usually unremarkable features were transformed by anger. His lips had thinned out to a tight, narrow line beneath flaring nostrils and taut-stretched cheeks. The deep-set brown eyes, previously mild and slightly sad, blazed with controlled anger and between them a band of scar tissue stood out white against the tan of his face.

She tried to turn her head away, but the fingers hooked around her jaw held her like a vice. Involuntarily, she shuddered.

'You ever try that again,' the voice was cold, flat and dangerous, 'and I'll kill you. Understand?'

She grunted her agreement and felt relief flood through her as the mask of fury above her slowly resolved back into Jubal's normal visage. He let her head go and she fell back on to the bunk, panting her fear.

Jubal decided to rely upon the effect of his anger to keep her under control: constant surveillance would be difficult and he could hardly keep her tied up. Better, then, to impress upon her the possible consequences of disobedience and trust to her fear to keep her in line.

'Finish dressing,' he said coldly, 'and no more tricks.'

Perhaps it was the prostitute's mentality that made her obey, or perhaps she had been so genuinely terrified that she was scared for her life, but Jubal had no more trouble throughout the journey. Instead, it passed quietly, almost amicably, falling into a four-day routine of meals, whistle-stops and conversation. Jubal learned a good deal about Victoria Kennedy as the thirty-five ton locomotive hauled its load northwards through Idaho and Oregon.

By the time they reached their jumping-off point at Black's Town, they were almost friends.

Black's Town consisted of a platform flanked by a tiny ticket office, a sprawl of one-storey, solid-looking timber houses and a couple of stores. There was a rooming house which they checked into as man and wife – Jubal did not yet trust Victoria sufficiently to risk giving her her own room – and a small livery stable.

They ate in the hotel, poor fare after the catering of the Union Pacific, and retired to their room. Jubal locked the door and pocketed the key, then, wrapped in a blanket, he settled down to sleep in the only armchair. The woman took the big double bed, inviting Jubal – not for the first time – to join her, but accepting his refusal with good enough grace. They woke cold and hungry and Jubal worked the pot-bellied stove in the centre of the room to new life as Victoria shivered beneath the sheets. When the stove was heated up they dressed and went out to breakfast.

While they ate, Jubal enquired about horses and, on the hotel owner's suggestion, walked Victoria down the single street to the stable. He purchased two horses together with riding tackle and led the animals back towards one of the general stores. There he bought suitable clothing for the woman, enough supplies to last them for a week and more information.

Deliverance lay about thirty miles due north across the Columbia River, perched in a hollow of the high-winding Cascades.

'That's bad country up there, friend,' warned the storekeeper, 'high timber an' not too many trails. Ain't hardly the kind of land to take a woman.'

Jubal smiled and made reassuring noises as he waited for Victoria to emerge from the room at the back. When she did, she was dressed in a divided broadcloth riding skirt with a woollen shirt and a leather jacket, a smile decorating her face.

'You know,' she said as they left the store, 'you've bought

me more new clothes in a week than anyone else did month.'

'Like that man I knew would say,' Jubal answered h smile, 'clothes maketh the man. Guess the same goes fo women.'

'I kinda go for you,' Victoria murmured, 'an' you can make me any time.'

'Thanks, ma'am,' Jubal replied, 'but right now I got other things on my mind.'

Victoria didn't answer, but the smile dimmed a little and she mounted her bay gelding in silence.

Ten hours later Jubal understood what the storekeeper had meant about the Cascades. He had climbed steadily all day, picking his way through pine breaks and rock falls, dismounting frequently to haul his pony bodily over the more difficult sections, and they could still see the lights of Black's Town below them. In ten hours' hard riding they had come, Jubal estimated, about eight miles. The calendar he had bought told him that he had two days to go if he was to meet Sillers' schedule for the meeting. With Deliverance still more than twenty miles away into the Cascades, they would have to make better time the next day.

They did, rising at dawn and eating a hurried breakfast before saddling the horses and pushing on into the mountains. As they approached the upper ranges, the terrain flattened out a little, so that the going became easier, the rock slides giving way to flat spaces of high pasture land where bighorn skittered nervously from their coming.

They made camp, tired and saddlesore, as night was coming down. Jubal could feel the cold weather nearing and wondered how much longer it would be before the north-country winter set in. Having experienced the snow-time of the Colorado plains, he had no wish to be caught so high and far north by the cold weather. He built a fire and settled on to his saddle blanket as Victoria began to cook. Whore she might b thought Jubal, but she certainly knew how to prepare foo When they had finished he stretched back, wrapped ir blanket, resting his head on his saddle and fell swiftly

93

sleep. He didn't think Victoria would try to get away and even if she did, she couldn't go far.

In the event, she fulfilled Jubal's trust: he woke up to the smell of coffee boiling over a new-kindled fire, vying with the bacon crackling in the pan and the fresh, green odour of pine.

It was a clear, cool, high-country morning, the fresh air and the pine trees combining to invigorate them both. The horses too were refreshed and ready to go and they made good time throughout the day, stopping only once to eat before heading onwards through the timberland. They made camp near a clear-water freshet that offered them both a chance to bathe and fill the canteens. It was, Jubal thought as he settled down to sleep, a far cry from their journey together over the Great Salt Lake.

At noon the next day they reached Deliverance.

The town huddled in a bowl of surrounding mountains, commanding the approach path of two rivers. It was surprisingly large, about one hundred and fifty buildings clustering up the riverbanks and slopes with scattered farms dotting the upland grass. A timber mill stood off to one side, throwing a tall column of black smoke high into the clear air. Jubal could hear the high-pitched scream of a chain saw bouncing off the slopes as they rode on to the trail leading into town. It wound down, steep and slippery, to the mainstreet, cutting between timbered cabins and smallholdings until the residential properties gave way to stores and saloons.

Jubal headed for the nearest hotel, a two-storey construction of solid pinewood and shingled roof. Victoria told him she had stayed there once with Sillers, and it seemed as good a choice as any. He checked them into a double room and carried their gear upstairs to a surprisingly spacious apartment at the front of the house, overlooking the street. Leaning out of the big window, Jubal could see three saloons and two restaurants; more than he had expected, but then again, he reminded himself, he had not expected Deliverance to be so large. Whatever was that held the inhabitants to the high country, it must be profitable to permit a town of that size.

He waited until Victoria had cleaned up and changed out of

her travelling clothes into the demure gingham dress and then pulled on a clean shirt and set out to find an eating house.

They chose the second they came to, a quiet place that was only partially occupied by townsfolk and lumberjacks. After they had finished, Jubal spent the remainder of the afternoon looking around the place. The centre of Deliverance had been planned carefully along a straight line that divided the ground between the two rivers. High-standing boardwalks flanked the buildings, sheltered from the sky above by weatherboarding roofs that ran in two continuous lines down both sides of the street. Side roads ran off at right angles to the twin rivers and the buildings beyond, reached across two timber bridges that looked solid enough to withstand the heaviest winter floods. Beyond, the periphery of the town spread in concentric circles up the slopes, the buildings becoming progressively smaller as they reached higher. The timber mill was located about half a mile to the south where the wind would carry the smoke of its machinery away to the east.

Jubal familiarized himself with the place and then returned to the hotel.

Victoria explained that on earlier visits Sillers had made contact with Beauregard's men in a saloon called the Lazy Dog. Evening was closing in, so they went to eat before heading for the saloon.

Jubal optioned a table towards the rear where they could see anyone coming in through the swing doors and ordered whisky. At first, the barman objected to Victoria's presence.

'We don't cater fer no ladies,' he grunted, 'ain't that kinda place.'

'You got a short memory, Charley,' replied Victoria, 'it wasn't that long ago you were trying to shove your hand up my skirt.'

'Mizz Vicky!' Charley was dumbfounded. 'I shore didn't recognize you. What you done to yoreself?'

'Got respectable,' answered Victoria shortly, 'but I still want a drink.'

'Why sure, Mizz Vicky,' grinned the barkeep, 'comin' right up.'

As a result of Victoria's presence, Jubal got the good whiskey and settled down to wait. The place filled as the night grew darker; lumbermen arrived in groups, jostling noisily with storekeepers and farmers, so that the Lazy Dog was gradually filled with smoke and the sound of voices. Card games were started and Jubal felt the familiar itch to join in, but resisted in favour of maintaining his vigilance.

He had been there for two hours and was returning from the bar with fresh glasses when it paid off.

A tall man wearing a faded grey jacket with the memory of epaulets still attached to the shoulders was standing over Victoria's chair. As Jubal approached, he reached out to grab her wrist, twisting it cruelly back against her shoulder. Jubal set the glasses down on the nearest table and walked over to the girl.

'Let her go.' His voice sounded conversational.

The man turned around and Jubal saw that he had only one eye. His right was covered by a large black patch, from beneath which a long scar extended down his cheek, bisecting his lips and disappearing in amongst the beard stubble decorating his chin.

The single eye glittered as he studied Jubal. 'What the hell d'you mean?'

Jubal recognized the southern accent and, at the same time, his eye spotted the man's gun. It was holstered on his right hip in a flapped, military rig with the butt pointing forwards, the way Tyree's men had carried their hand weapons.

'I mean you should leave her be,' replied Jubal in the same even tone, 'because she's with me and I don't like to see women manhandled.'

'Too fuckin' bad,' snarled one-eye as he lunged forwards.

Jubal was ready to fight, but the speed of the big man's attack was still surprising. He spread his arms wide and flung them around Jubal, a fist smashed against his chest, but he ignored it as he picked Jubal up in a bear hug, and swung him round in a tight, dancing circle.

Jubal felt the wind driven from his lungs as his arms were pinned to his sides and his feet left the floor. Victoria screamed and rose to her feet, but a second grey-jacketed man grabbed her, holding her still as a ring cleared around the two combatants. The tall man's height gave him the advantage, for he was able to hold Jubal in the air as he crushed the smaller man, bending him remorselessly backwards. Jubal knew that he had to escape the killing embrace before lack of oxygen blacked him out, or his spine snapped, but he could not use his hands or even gain the swing for a kick.

Instead, he nodded sharply forwards, driving his skull hard against the other's nose. He heard a yell and felt blood spatter his face as the grip loosened. It gave him the chance to pull one arm free. He lifted up and back and drove his flattened palm directly on to the man's bleeding nose. He felt it pulp under the blow, the bridge crushing into a soggy tissue of bone and mangled flesh. Then he was free and falling to the floor.

He landed on his feet, using his left hand to grab the wrist swinging towards him. He pivoted to the right, dragging the man's arm up and over his shoulder as he hooked his right forearm over the wrist and dragged down. Swung forwards by the momentum of his blow, the big man toppled off balance, seesawing on Jubal's shoulder before he rose into the air and flew over Jubal's head.

The smaller man held on to the wrist, so that as his attacker landed on his back, his right arm was held at the wrist over the pivot of Jubal's forearm. The limb broke with a clear, sharp *click*, the jagged ends of bone spiking up through the soft flesh of his underarm.

He screamed, high and shrill like a wounded pig, until Jubal's boot smashed against the side of his neck.

Jubal whirled, conscious of someone moving up behind him. As he turned, he saw a circle of grey-clad men watching grimly, one of them coming forwards with a ·36 Spiller and Burr revolver lifting out of the reversed holster.

Pure instinct took over as Jubal continued to turn, letting himself fall to the right as his hand lifted to the shoulder holster beneath his jacket. His fingers closed around the butt while he was still falling, hauling the ·30 calibre Colt free so that he hit the floor with the hammer back and his finger pulling on the trigger.

The bullet hit at close range while the other man was still cocking the percussion gun, blasting into his midriff so that he doubled over, driven backwards by the power of the shell. He spread blood in a fan over the boots of the onlookers as he hit the sawdust and rolled over. Pain was inscribed in every line on his face as he pushed to his knees, still thumbing at the hammer.

Jubal lay prone on the floor, cocked the Colt and shot the man a second time. The bullet hit him between the eyes, snapping his head back in a frothy fountain of blood and brain matter as his gun ploughed splinters from the planking. He rested in a kneeling position for several seconds, tears trickling from dead eyes in a stream that mingled with the crimson flood welling from the third hole in his forehead, then he slumped forwards and lay still.

Jubal was rising to his feet when something hit his wrist, smashing the Colt from his hand. He tried to reach it, but something else exploded inside his head and the room spun in front of him. Dimly, through a big, black haze that was clouding out the figures surrounding him, he heard Victoria's voice.

'You wanted to meet Beauregard's people. Say hallo.'

'I guess,' mumbled Jubal as his head hit the floor, 'that we'll save the formal introductions for later.'

# CHAPTER TEN

The man facing Jubal was white as a ghost, his face the pale colour of bleached bone, its pallor disturbed only by the pink-rimmed eyes that bore like a demon's gaze into Jubal's. His shoulder-length hair, falling free beneath the white-feathered, side-buttoned hat he wore, was as death-white as his face.

He was dressed in a faded, but crisply-pressed, grey jacket decorated with gold trimmings around the collar and cuffs. His pants matched the grey of his gold-buttoned jacket and his boots shone bright in the morning sun, setting off the glint of the sabre slung on his left hip.

He smiled, very pale and very evil, as he studied Jubal's face.

'Let me introduce myself. I am General Beauregard.'

Jubal might have answered, but a bayonet was stuck between his teeth, lashed in position with a length of cord that held the razor-sharp blade tight against his tongue. He could not remove it because his wrists were tied above his head, secured to the limb of an overhanging tree, so that he swung with his toes barely touching the ground, unable to move.

He was abruptly conscious of the sun on his back, and as the fog in his head cleared he realized that he was stripped to the waist.

'I understand,' murmured the albino in a soft Southern drawl, 'that you killed one of my men and crippled another. Captain Stewart, I am told, will lose the full use of the arm you broke. I cannot permit such wanton deprivation.' He paused, his red eyes fixed on Jubal's face. 'So, whatever your motives in coming here, I have to punish you.'

He looked over Jubal's shoulder and nodded.

As the brim of the grey stetson fell, Jubal felt raw fire burst across his back. Instinctively, he started to shout, but the edge of the bayonet, drawing blood from his tongue, stopped him.

The pain lashed his spine a second time and he fought for the control he needed to prevent him from lacerating his tongue. He clamped his teeth on the blade and tried hard to brace his body as the third stroke fell. It was difficult: the pain of the whip was too great; the threat of the bayonet too immediate. But somehow he endured.

It continued for twenty strokes; how long they lasted, Jubal could not tell; all he knew was that the pain ceased after a while, the dancing devil's fire across his back ceasing, to leave only the numbing miasma of half-conscious cessation of pain.

Faint through the tears clouding his eyes he saw the white-faced figure of Beauregard as he heard, through the ringing in his ears, the man's voice.

'Consider yourself lucky, Dr. Cade. We are not permitted to flog a soldier in the Confederate Army, but as you are a civilian, we could not brand you.'

The ropes hitching Jubal to the tree were cut and he fell heavily on to the ground at Beauregard's feet.

Dimly, he was conscious of a bright-polished boot tip lifting his chin, of eyes the colour of cold red fire staring down at him and the voice that sounded like the North Wind telling someone to drag him away and check his wounds. He felt hands grasp his ankles and the salty taste of blood in his mouth, then the rasp of grass under his chest as he was dragged away. Dirt clogged his teeth as he bumped roughly over the ground, his eyes fixed on the tall figure striding, oblivious to the punishment he had ordered, away from the bleeding man being hauled like a slaughtered animal across the camp site.

Jubal felt hands lifting him and voices, obscure through the waves of grey pain flooding his mind, discussing his condition.

'Jesus, Bob. You ever see a flogging like that?'

'Cain't say as I did, Jimmy. But then ole General Beau' allus did have a hankerin' fer discipline.'

'Godawmity, man, that weren't no *military* floggin', that was damn' near pure murder. You ever see a man whipped with a bayonet 'tween his teeth?'

'Cain't say as I have. But then again I ain't never seen no one bust up Stewart's arm an' gut-shoot Hanna. Until this little mother came on the scene.'

Jubal felt a boot nudge his ribs as the last speaker finished his sentence. He bit off the cry of pain that rose to his lips and concentrated on keeping quiet and listening to their conversation.

'Shit, don't hurt him no more.' The speaker was a fat man carrying sergeant's stripes on his arm. 'He's had enough fer anyone.'

'All right, Sarge. I'll leave him be.' The other was a younger soldier, wearing corporal's chevrons on the sleeve of his grey jacket. 'Don't reckon he'll last the night out anyways.'

'I ain't sure,' said the fat man, 'I got a feelin' this one'll be around a while. I never seen a man take a floggin' like that before. An' he's still breathin'. So you jest keep an eye on 'im.'

Jubal was inside a tent, insulated against the colding weather with a thick layer of straw spread over a waterproof groundsheet, the central pole rose five feet up to the cone of the dirty white canvas walls, so that his guard stooped as he watched the plump sergeant stride off through the orderly rows of matching bivouacs. It was obvious that the youngster did not realize that Jubal was conscious; he waited until the older man was gone from sight and then squatted, with a weary sigh, on to the straw.

When Jubal spoke, he jumped; visibly.

'What the hell are you?' The words came thick through the pain constricting Jubal's throat. 'Who's Beauregard?'

Startled, the soldier answered without thinking. 'Seventeenth Tennessee. Other regiments affiliated. Shit!' He recognized that his prisoner was not only alive, but also still thinking. 'Why'd you want ter know?'

Jubal tried hard to push away the waves of pain drifting through his body and concentrate on forming his questions; and at the same time on giving the man in grey the answers he wanted.

'I came a long way to deliver a message. I'd like to see it get through. Beauregard could be grateful.'

'One more hired word-carrier, heh?' The corporal puffed a

gobbet of chewing tobacco close to Jubal's head. 'Like ole Sillers. Allus carryin' messages, like how difficult it was to get the guns up here, an' how the beef wouldn't be on time.'

He paused to cut a fresh wad from the black swatch in his breast pocket. He pushed a chunk of the stuff into his mouth and chewed thoughtfully before he continued.

'Tyree got the goods, awright. Tyree was a man you could trust.'

Jubal took the opportunity to break in.

'Tyree trusted me with a message.' He did his best to say it clearly around the pain. 'It was Tyree asked me to find Beauregard and give him the message.'

The corporal was shocked, it was obvious from the way his mouth gaped open, allowing a trickle of tobacco-stained saliva to dribble out down his chin.

'Tyree give you a message for General Beau'?'

'Corporal, you better believe it.' Jubal was anxious to make as much capital as he could: given his present position, he needed it. 'And what he told me is for Beauregard's ears only.'

The corporal was gone before Jubal could begin to elaborate further on his story, jumping to his feet in a panic-stricken spray of half-chewed tobacco as he lurched out of the tent. Jubal watched him go, peering through the open flap as he lay on his stomach, trying hard to ignore the fiery pain of the lacerations across his back.

He could not tell how long it was before Beauregard appeared, stepping smartly through the tent's opening as the corporal held back the flap.

The albino stood straight as a ramrod over Jubal, eyeing the wounds criss-crossing the prisoner's back.

'I understand you have something to tell me.' His voice was deep-South cultured; slow, lazy and mean. 'I believe you undertook to deliver a message.'

'That's right.' Jubal was resenting his position on the floor of the tent. 'From one of your . . . *helpers*?' He emphasized the last word. 'He asked me to pass it on. Before he died.'

'And what would that be?' Beauregard remained as white and cool as an iceberg.

'Untie me, give me some clothes, and I might feel like talking.' Jubal was feeling angry, even through the pain tracing his back.

It was a hard-hat gamble, but it paid off, because Beauregard spun on one well-polished bootheel and barked an order to the soldier waiting outside the tent.

'Corporal!' His voice was cold as his dead, red eyes. 'Get a medic to this man. See that he's attended to. Then get him dressed and ready to present in my bivouac.'

He turned without looking again at Jubal, and marched out of the tent.

Moments later a skinny youngster appeared clutching a roll of bandage and a tin of antiseptic cream. He was by no means sure of what he was doing, and once he realized that Jubal had professional training, was happy to sit back and listen to the instructions coming from his patient.

'Hell, doc,' he explained. 'No one ever tole me about medickin'. I jest got appointed on account of how I'm a lousy shot. General Beau', he jest needed someone to tie bandages an' the like. Not that there's been too much need o' that lately. We ain't been in a good fight fer at least two months.'

Jubal wondered, as the salve was rubbed into his back, exactly what these soldiers were doing in the Cascade mountains. From their speech and their uniforms, it was obvious that they were Confederates; from the lists he had read in Sillers' wagon, it was obvious they were still active. But the Civil War had ended years ago.

So why were they still operative?

He was trying to figure it out when the fat sergeant reappeared, fidgeting just inside the tent until the young medic had completed his bandaging of Jubal's whiplashed back.

'Kin you stand?' He sounded almost apologetic. 'The Gen'ral wants to see you.'

Jubal climbed to his feet, pulling on his shirt despite the pain. He kept the sergeant waiting while he donned his jacket and derby, then followed the fat man through the tent village, until they reached a big, plank-fronted bivouac.

Inside, snow-white head bent over a desk, he could see

Beauregard studying a spread of papers. The sergeant coughed, so that the red-eyed commander looked up, briefly irritated by the interruption. Then he spotted Jubal and ushered his prisoner in. Jubal stepped up on to the planking that floored the big tent, watching the albino as he walked inside.

'Sit down,' murmured Beauregard.

'Thanks,' answered Jubal, staring back at the man's inflamed pupils, 'that's white of you.'

# CHAPTER ELEVEN

'You'd best explain your presence, Dr. Cade.' Beauregard's voice was stone-cold formal, his diction, beneath the Southern drawl, cuttingly precise: like a judge pronouncing the death sentence.

'I was asked to deliver a message.' Jubal matched the military man's formality.

'By Sillers?'

'No, Tyree. I found him dying and promised to take a message to Canfield.'

'I understand that both Canfield and Sillers are dead.' Despite the sunlight filtering into the open tent, Beauregard's eyes never blinked as they studied Jubal's face. 'How did they die?'

Jubal was unsure how much the albino knew, and for no particular reason he felt it would be better to keep quiet about his acquaintanceship with Ahab, so he shrugged vaguely. 'I'm not sure. Sillers was shot at long range. That's about all I know.'

'And Tyree?' Beauregard's eyes were like gimlets.

'Like I said, I found him dying after an Apache raid. He said you'd lost the guns and cattle and he gave me a parcel to deliver.'

Beauregard threw the packet on to the desk in front of him as Jubal finished speaking. The contents spread out fan-wise over the rough wood, but the soldier didn't look at the papers, just kept staring into Jubal's eyes.

'Did you understand them?'

Jubal saw little point in denying that he had read the documents. 'No, I didn't. I had to read them to find you.'

Beauregard snorted. Jubal could not tell whether it was in disgust or from relief; the man's bone-white face gave little away.

'Dr. Cade,' he murmured thoughtfully, 'I have an offer to

make you. An offer you can't refuse. I can use a qualified doctor. Oh, I know more about you than you realize,' a faint smile divided his thin lips for a moment, 'the woman told me all about you and I intend to ... shall we say, *recruit* you? In return for your life you will agree to act as medical officer to the regiment. It seems a fair compromise. After all,' he paused, toying with the hilt of his sabre, 'if you reject the offer I shall have no alternative but to kill you. And the woman, of course.'

As though on cue, two troopers wearing grey uniforms topped off by slope-fronted grey forage caps, dragged a tearful Victoria into the tent. Beauregard rose as she was hauled in, ducking his snow-white head in a travesty of good manners.

'Don't trust him, Jubal!' It was a plaintive cry that broke off abruptly as Beauregard's right fist landed across her mouth.

The general stood before her, his eyes fixed on Jubal, waiting for an answer with a grim smile decorating his face. It was the kind of smile that said he had never doubted the outcome of his suggestion, that he held Jubal like a puppet in his long-fingered hands. Jubal hated it. He hated Beauregard. But he couldn't envisage any alternative but to accept the proposal; he was not ready to die, nor did he wish to see the woman die. And he had no doubts at all but that Beauregard meant every word he said.

'All right,' he nodded, 'I'll accept.'

'Excellent.' Beauregard smiled like a death's-head, his stark face dividing to show teeth the same colour as his skin. 'Show the medical officer his quarters.'

The soldiers holding the unconscious Victoria hurried to obey. Jubal was led through the encampment to a large tent situated close to the central ring of concentric canvas circles and ushered inside by a trooper clearly unsure of his position in the military hierarchy. At least it gave him a degree of privacy and the opportunity to settle Victoria on a camp bed away from the lustful eyes of the grey-uniformed soldiers. The rifle-carrying guard at the opening was something he intended to worry about later on.

Briskly, he checked the tent. It was stocked efficiently,

carrying in numerous lockers the medical supplies necessary to the care of the thousand-odd soldiers he estimated were under Beauregard's strange command. He racked his brains to remember what he knew about military formations; from distant memories of newspaper reports back in England, he seemed to recall that a regiment at full strength consisted of something over 1,500 men. Beauregard appeared to be commanding at least a full-strength regiment of Confederate soldiers.

Why was something Jubal intended to find out.

He got the chance the next morning, when the young corporal who had helped drag him from the whipping tree appeared, complaining of stomach cramps. Jubal administered medicine and discreet questions in equal measures, learning as he doled out the enema that Beauregard's command was made up of soldiers from various Southern commands. Squadrons of cavalry bivouacked with artillery men, backed by troops of infantry and engineers.

When Jubal pointed out that the Civil War was long finished, the soldier laughed in his face.

Fifteen minutes later, he was hauled before Beauregard.

The commanding officer's face was cold as a bad winter and his voice hit Jubal like the wind off the high plains.

'Cade.' Jubal noticed the *doctor* was gone. 'Your task was to administer to medical needs, not ask questions. You've asked one too many. From now on you are confined to the stockade.'

Spittle flecked Beauregard's lips and a deadly light played in the pink of his eyes. Jubal was not sure how far he could go in safety, for by now he was convinced of the general's insanity, but none the less decided to push a point.

'You wanted a doctor, right?' He tried to keep his voice even, placatory. 'I was doctoring. I asked a few questions; that's only natural, after all.'

Beauregard came from behind the desk in a stiff-legged rush that brought him face to face with the smaller man. His eyes glowed with an unholy light as his mouth spat words like bullets at Jubal's ears.

'*I am set over the nations and over the kingdoms, to root*

*out, to build, and to plant. To destroy and throw down.* And on the ashes rebuild a nation that should not have gone down into ignomity. The words are those of the prophet Jeremiah, Cade. I intend to see that they apply to the South; to rebuild our heritage; replenish our power. The Yankees have trodden us down too long. I shall change that.'

Jubal recognized the biblical quotation as the one Canfield had used in his sermon, and he detected in Beauregard's voice the same fanatic tones, simultaneously compelling and terrifying. Whatever mad cause the man pursued, he obviously believed in it to the exclusion of rationality.

'General,' Jubal said softly, 'the Civil War is over. The South lost and now it's pretty well rebuilt. I've been down there and I can tell you: no one's fighting any more.'

He broke off as Beauregard came to his feet, one hand raised in a peremptory gesture for silence.

'Cade.' The voice was as flat as a diamondback's stare, and every bit as dangerous. *'The war is not over.* It will not be over until I have won back our heritage. Lee may have been forced to surrender at Appomattox, but I signed no filthy treaty, nor shall I. Oh no, I shall fight on.' Spittle ran frothy over the paleness of his unbearded chin. 'I shall fight and win, because now that the nigger-lover Lincoln is dead, thanks to a brave patriot, I have only that drunken sot Grant to deal with.'

Jubal had never heard John Wilkes Booth described as a patriot before, although he had heard rumours of Grant's capacity for whiskey. He had met diehard Southerners before, but never one quite so convincingly deadly as the red-eyed man before him. He kept his mouth shut and listened.

'And Grant,' Beauregard went on, 'happens to be walking at this very moment into my hands. President Grant,' he spat the words, 'intends to visit Washington. When he does,' he paused, savouring the dramatic effect of his words, *'I intend to kill him.'*

As he finished the sentence, he stepped towards Jubal. Instinctively, the smaller man backed away, dropping to a defensive crouch. He had anticipated the attack, but not the form it would take: Beauregard's arm lifted as though to strike, and

Jubal brought up his left arm to ward off the blow, at the same time powering his body forwards, right fist swinging at the Southerner's belly. As he moved, a heavy blow sent pain radiating from the lash marks on his back, so that he was smashed to the plank floor of the tent. He was trying to get up when a rifle butt jarred the teeth in his head and dizzy waves of nausea dropped him back to the boards. A third blow bounced his face off the floor and he lost consciousness.

He came to in semi-darkness, suddenly aware of a bearded face hovering over him. He tried to rise, but powerful hands held him down as a deep voice rang through the misty memories that fogged his mind.

'Take it easy, friend. You're alright now.'

'Yeah?' Jubal stretched back on to what appeared to be a camp bed. 'Where the hell am I?'

'In the stockade.' The speaker's face came into focus, revealing tired green eyes, deep-set in a thin face, so undernourished that the cheek-bones stood out like tombstones above a thick growth of black beard. He wore a ragged, dirty blue jacket decorated across the shoulders with what was left of a captain's gold bars. 'I'm Newman, lately a captain in the Fourteenth Cavalry. U.S. Army, of course. Right now I'm one more prisoner of that madman Beauregard.'

He paused and spat as Jubal sat up, becoming aware, as his eyes grew accustomed to the dusky gloom, of two other men standing watching him. Newman caught his gaze and turned to look over his shoulder.

'Meet Pickett an' Nicholls.'

A six-foot plus Negro wearing faded sergeant's stripes and the signs of dysentery flashed white teeth in Jubal's direction. Beside him, a middle-aged man with wavy grey hair and a sailor-suit lifted a hand in brief greeting.

'Pickett served with my squadron until we got caught,' Newman explained. 'Nicholls was on a boat running supplies into Aberdeen until he found out who they were for. After that he ended up here.'

'Bloody right.' Jubal recognized the seaman's West Country accent; he was, presumably, off an English boat. 'If I'd known what we were doing, I'd never have signed on.'

'Ain't no use in weepin' over wasted cargo,' murmured Pickett, his black face greying as the bugs in his stomach fought the dark pigmentation of his skin, 'the problem we got us right now is gettin' outta here an' stoppin' Beauregard.'

'Preferably dead,' added Newman.

Jubal pushed himself up off the bed. His head ached abominably from the butt-stroking and his back hurt from the whipping, but he sensed an urgency about his three companions that inflamed further his own concern with Beauregard's parting comments.

'Exactly what *is* going on here?' he demanded.

Newman took a deep breath and began to explain.

Lieutenant-General Mordecai Nathaniel Beauregard had won himself a reputation in the Civil War as one of the Confederate States' most ardent defenders. The right to own slaves, the right of the Southern States to secede from the Union, the justice of their cause, were all matters close to his heart. He had proved his beliefs in the way he fought. Rising fast from a relatively junior cavalry commander, renowned for his savagely unorthodox skirmishing tactics, he had won battlefield commissions at Manassas (First Bull Run to the North), Fredericksburg and Chancellorsville. At Gettysburg, he had held his men together in a last-ditch stand against the Union that had won him his General's stars. He had excelled at Brice's Cross Roads and then joined with Jubal early in the Confederate push up the Shenandoah Valley.

Sherman's march through Georgia had stripped him clean of every parcel of land he owned, and after the reversal of Jubal's Raid, he had followed the Moseby trail to guerrilla tactics. Commanding a mixed bag of cavalry, infantry and artillery, he had been ordered to drop out of the Eastern theatre of war in order to set up a striking force in the Union rear.

With a full regiment under his command, Beauregard had set sail from Charleston, bound for Aberdeen in Washington. The strategy was unorthodox, but brilliant, designed to establish a Confederate fighting force far behind Northern lines, where it might stab the Union's back and persuade the cotton-hungry, British-influenced Canadians to join the war. Britain and Canada, however, had chosen to play both ends of the game: cotton was traded, and more than one Confederate warship had slid down the ramp of a British builder's yard, but neither country had made a firm alliance.

The net result was that Beauregard had been left alone to play the guerrilla game. Like Moseby and, to a more violent extent, Quantrill, he had pursued a policy of hit-and-run fighting. Since 1865, when the Old South fell for ever, he had existed on a tenuous linkage of sympathizers and profiteers. Fanatics like Tyree and Canfield had kept him supplied with food, guns and information; profiteers like Sillers had greased the wheels and their own palms. Now a new element intruded upon the crazy situation. The North-western areas were wide open to industrial expansion. The timber-lined hills and ore-rich ridges promised huge profits to the businessmen back East; to extract the riches stored in the Cascades, railroads were necessary. And railroads spelled money.

With the Confederate Government gone for ever, Beauregard had suddenly found new backers in the unscrupulous bankers of 'civilized' America.

He had been able to continue his campaign of guerrilla raiding, slowly building a mountain empire that promised to overthrow the appointed government of the United States.

His Eastern contacts had forewarned him of Grant's visit. The railroad question was one that troubled the Senate, so riddled was it with internecine politics, profiteering and outright chicanery. The result was that the President himself had decided to take a look at first hand. He was due within the month, that had been the purpose of Tyree's shipment, for Beauregard planned an attack that would rob America of its leader.

'That's why,' Newman concluded, 'we have to get out of here. There's no one can warn Grant, 'ceptin' us. Beauregard's got at least five 32-pounders ready to hit the train, along with infantry and cavalry. If we can't pass the word, then Grant's deader'n a plucked turkey at the county fair.'

111

Jubal looked out of the tent at the high, palisaded walls of the stockade. It was constructed around a square, with Gatling guns commanding the four right-angles of the walls and armed guards patrolling the outer perimeters. Beyond the guns and the guards spread the pennants of the camp; and farther out, the timbered slopes of the Cascades, high, wild wilderness land.

'An animal could do it,' he murmured, 'so we got to think like animals. And one way or another, we got to get out of this place.'

# CHAPTER TWELVE

Jubal had been in the stockade for ten days and still hadn't figured a way to get out. Newman and Pickett had been there for three months, ever since their patrol got too close to the Confederate hide-out and Beauregard massacred all but the two survivors. Nicholls had been imprisoned when he protested against the destination of his ship's cargo: he had been given charge of a shore party and after talking with a lieutenant had realized that he was delivering weapons to an illegal army. The operation was, Jubal decided, financed by business interests as widely spread as they were influential; it had to be, there was no other way the regiment could exist, even in the wilderness of the Cascades.

He had tried talking to the guards and got a rifle butt in his stomach: fraternization was forbidden; the penalty: branding.

Consequently, the thirty prisoners Beauregard was holding hostage as a bargaining force were unable to persuade their captors that the war was long over. The rebels, anyway, were die-hard fanatics, as fervent in their love of the South's cause as the general himself. The hostages were held incommunicado, their only contacts the stone-faced men patrolling the confines of their prison. Food was brought once a day and dumped in the no-man's land between outer and inner gates, medicine was non-existent and until Jubal's arrival doctoring had been a makeshift practice of half-remembered knowledge backed up by guesswork.

Newman's awareness of the Confederate plan came from his own interview with Beauregard and a rebel officer. The man had been thrown into the stockade three-quarters dead from a beating. He had learned that the war was over and expressed a desire to return home; Beauregard had ordered his flogging as an example to morale. Before the man died – they had never

113

learned his name – he told Newman what was going on.

It amazed Jubal that so great a secret could be kept – until he saw how tightly Beauregard controlled his command.

'Hell, Jubal,' remarked Newman bitterly when the question came up, 'we're thirty miles from the nearest town an' that's populated by sympathizers. The only men who ever leave camp outside of the raiding parties are half-crazy officers who'd ride Beauregard's coat-tails into hell if he told them to. We're sittin' on a powder keg with a lit fuse, an' our hands are tied.'

It was the cavalryman's last embittered remark that gave Jubal the idea. They began to put it into operation that day.

There were thirty men in the stockade, mostly Union soldiers with a sprinkling of miners and local homesteaders opposed to Beauregard's plans. Four were dying slowly, wasted by chronic dysentery; five more were too weak to be any use. That gave Jubal twenty-two almost able-bodied men to use: poor odds against a well armed regiment. But they agreed to try, anyway.

Throughout the day they gathered brushwood from the thickets sprouting within the walls of their prison, claiming it was in preparation for the cold weather. Come nightfall, they silently struck the seven tents given them by the rebels. Four carefully hoarded knives were produced and the canvas cut into strips. Then they lashed the brushwood into several bundles and settled down to wait for full dark. It was a moonless night, scudding clouds obscuring the thin crescent of the new moon, so that they were able to move close to the perimeter undetected. Fifteen men were detailed to act as an assault party, the remaining seven assigned to carry the brushwood.

The seven pushed their bundles up against the walls of the stockade and fired the dry wood.

It caught fast, sending long tongues of flame up the dry walls of the palisades to lick around the platforms supporting the Gatling guns.

Taken by surprise, the drowsy guards failed to open fire immediately. The short delay gave Jubal's men the time they needed to mount an attack, volleying rocks through the fires so that the machine-gunners ducked and dodged in confusion. It gave five men a chance to scale the walls, ignoring the flames searing their clothing and flesh. Spurred on by the hate nurtured over the months of their confinement, they hit the gun positions with berserk fury. One fell back, his skull shattered by an officer's bullet as the Gatling chattered blindly over the stockade. One hurled himself over the revolving cylinder of the second gun, his body spreading in ragged tatters of ruptured flesh over the faces of the men below. But his dead fingers clung to the barrels, pulling the gun down so that others could climb up and haul it from the platform.

Three more hit a gun in unison, smashing the three-man crew to the ground and pulling the Gatling round to bear on the two remaining guns. An artillery sergeant manned the trigger while a cavalry corporal fed the magazine and an infantry captain called targets.

The sergeant cranked the handle that rotated the ten barrels of the machine-gun, raking the nearest Confederate position with murderous glee. The rebels, concentrating on the prisoners below them, were taken by surprise. They were suddenly picked up and hurled from their platform by the hail of whistling death that hit them like a hammer. Their gun fell silent as they died, and more prisoners scaled the wall to man the temporarily silent death machine.

The fourth Gatling lifted its aim from the stockade to bear on the Union gun and for long moments the two weapons traded shells. The captain commanding the prisoners' gun took three rounds through the chest, lifting high into the air as the bullets plucked him from the platform and life. The corporal screamed as he felt his arm shatter, then picked up a fresh magazine and fed it into the gun with his left hand, ignoring the blood soaking his blue jacket. The sergeant crouched behind the Gatling, cranking and holding the trigger down.

Then the other Gatling came to life. From the angle of the walls it poured lead at the rebels. Caught between the two dancing, lancing columns of fire, the Confederates gave up. Two fell, riddled with bullets, while the gun captain threw himself bodily to the safety of the outer camp. As he hit the ground and rose, clutching a broken shoulder, Jubal headed a charge at the gates. Over his head, the two Gatlings directed their fire at the guards massing there. The Confederates scattered as the two guns, each capable of firing 400 rounds a minute, ploughed dirt, bone and blood from their ranks. They fell back, away from the gunfire and the flames blazing around the gate and the screaming column of angry men charging at them.

Jubal went through the flames like a demon leading a charge out through the gates of hell. A trooper too slow to get out of his way went down as Jubal ran straight into him. As they fell Jubal twisted so that he landed, shoulder first, on the man's chest. The rebel grunted as air was driven from his lungs, then tried to scream as Jubal's knee drove up into his groin. He doubled over, clutching at his pain, and Jubal took the chance to power to his feet and grab the man's rifle. Lifting it high, he brought it down in a savage arc that broke the Confederate's neck.

Behind him, the other escapers hit their former guards like human whirlwinds. Rifles were slapped aside by bare hands as the prisoners fell on the rebels. Like a wolf pack they rent and tore, venting their long-pent hate on the nearest representatives of their suffering.

Jubal hung on to the rifle and ran through the main camp, heading for Beauregard's tent.

All around him was confusion. The Confederates were emerging from their tents, bleary-eyed with sleep, shouting to one another as they tried to find out what was happening. Close to the stockades, tents were burning as the escaping prisoners threw torches at the canvas. The night was redolent of the stink of burning, noisy with shots and shouts, alive with running men. Now that they had obtained some weapons, the prisoners were forming a skirmish line under Newman's command, moving through the camp in the direction of the horse herd, shooting as they went.

It all served Jubal's purpose, giving him the chance he needed to move undetected through the camp. Dressed in his grey suit, clutching the rifle, he looked sufficiently like a rebel trooper to escape notice.

He made it as far as Beauregard's tent before he was spotted. A tall sergeant with a shock of red hair tumbling from under his cap came out with a Spencer pointed in Jubal's direction.

Alvin Tuohy had joined Beauregard's command back in 1864 when the – then – colonel had led a column up the Shenandoah. Alvin was Alabama born and raised and he knew where niggers belonged in society and what should be done with Union sympathizers. He had enjoyed watching the flogging of the little punk who had crippled his best friend, Stewart. The sight of so much pain being inflicted had given him a warm feeling in his gut that tightened his pants and prompted him to go looking for Keeley, the little drummer-boy. He'd left Keeley weeping like a girl and himself feeling a whole lot better and he hadn't had so much fun in weeks. Not since the raid on Breadsville, when he'd found the mayor's daughter hiding in the loft. The acquisition of the new prisoner's rifle had cheered him up even more. It was a handsome weapon, that converted, lever-action Spencer, a real accurate ·30 calibre death-dealer. He'd used it to threaten Keeley only yesterday, when the kid argued about taking another walk in the woods.

Now Alvin was facing the owner of the gun.

Jubal recognized it as Alvin worked the action. The red-haired bisexual wasn't quite used to the rifle and Jubal's looted Henry was cocked anyway, so he beat him.

The ·44 calibre slug spread Alvin's hopes of future conquests over the front of his trousers. Jubal worked the lever and corrected his aim: the next shot cut the redhead's shrill of pain off where it began as the 'Damn' Yankee' gun blew his lungs away. The muzzle was close enough that the velocity of the shell pushed Alvin backwards, walking him across the boards with his arms flapping through the curtain of blood he was spraying. Jubal levered the Henry and raked the tent with fire as he moved forwards, he kept shooting as Alvin pitched over through the entrance, then dropped the rifle and grabbed

117

his own gun.

He went in through the entrance with the Spencer cocked and ready, sliding over Alvin's blood as he powered himself inside.

'Don't shoot, mister! I'm just the drummer-boy.'

Keeley's potential problems about his future tastes were abruptly concluded as a bullet drove through his chest. He fell forwards over the corpse of his dead lover as Jubal jumped his body, propelling himself into the tent.

Beauregard's office was empty, but spread over a table to one side were the items Jubal wanted. He picked up his Colt, draping the holster over his left shoulder as he crammed cartridges into his pockets. The maps he had collected from Tyree went into an inside pocket, the saddlebags – still full of money – joined the Colt on his shoulder, and then he grabbed his medical valise in his left hand and turned to go.

As he turned, he saw Beauregard pointing a long-barrelled percussion revolver at his stomach. The albino was baring his teeth in a grimace halfway between a smile and a rictus. He was trembling with fury, but the hand holding the gun remained rock-steady.

'I should have killed you right off, Cade,' he snarled, 'shot you down like the Union-dog you are. I'll remedy that mistake right now.'

'No you won't, general.'

Jubal recognized the voice and, from the corner of his eye, saw Victoria Kennedy emerge from a screened-off section behind him. She was clad in a flimsy silk gown that exposed most of her impressive torso and was cut so that it fell away from her thighs, showing off the long, well-shaped columns of her legs. She was made up with all the garishness of a saloon whore, mascara painting dark shadows around her eyes, thrown into stark relief by the dead-white powder plastered over her face. Her lips stood out full and bright red against the artificial pallor that couldn't quite succeed in hiding the bruises decorating her cheeks and swollen lips.

She held her arms extended before her, levelling the .41 Derringer she clutched in the two-handed grip dead centre on

118

Beauregard's chest.

'You make one move to use that gun and I'll kill you.'

Jubal shifted slightly so that he could hold both Victoria and Beauregard within his field of vision. The woman saw him turn and smiled cynically.

'You see what he's done to me?' She wiggled her hips, fluttering the negligée clear of her legs so Jubal could see the ugly, red burn marks decorating her upper thighs. 'The general can't take a woman the normal way. He needs to hurt her to get his dander up. You smoke cigars, don't you, Jubal? The general don't smoke them, but he sure as hell uses them.'

Her voice broke in a sob of pain, anger and disgust. And Beauregard took advantage of her distress.

The pistol bucked in his hand, blowing a small red hole through the nipple of her left breast. Victoria screamed and fell backwards, discharging the tiny Derringer through the canvas above Beauregard's head. She was still on her way to the floor as Jubal fired. He was holding the Spencer in one hand and the shot was from the hip, but it still lifted threads of grey from Beauregard's uniform as the albino threw himself sideways.

He hit the planking and rolled, cocking the handgun as he tumbled. Simultaneously, Jubal threw his right hand down to work the Spencer's action, letting the rifle fall closed and cocked from its own weight, squeezing the trigger as the hammer clicked back.

The bullet burst splinters from the woodwork inches away from Beauregard's moving body and Jubal was steadying the gun for another shot as the rebel pushed himself out of the tent. His own shot went wide and then he was gone into the blazing night.

Jubal turned to Victoria, stooping over her as pain-filled eyes looked tearfully into his.

'He hurt me, Jubal,' she murmured, blood flecking her already bright lips, 'he hurt be mad.'

'You'll be O.K.' Jubal didn't mean it because he could see that she was dying; the bullet had gone too close to her heart. 'But we have to get out of here.'

119

'Not me.' Victoria's voice was slurred with pain. 'But you better move on. Pretty fast too. Before he comes back.' She smiled, lifting a hand to touch Jubal's face. 'You know something, Jubal? Apart from Roy Sillers, you're the only man ever treated me like a lady. I don't want to see you shot down, so get on outta here. Go through the back.'

Jubal nodded mutely and lowered her blonde head to the floor. She was dead before he left the tent.

He moved fast to the curtained area and lifted the bottom edge of the canvas, bellying out like a thief in the night. Sporadic firing shattered the mountain air as the prisoners moved towards the horses; running men filled the stillnesses between the bursts of gunfire with shouting, and all around the camp blazed as dry canvas took fire. The flames radiated outwards from the stockade, threatening soldiers and supplies alike. A large proportion of Beauregard's command was taken up with fighting the blaze, so Jubal succeeded in reaching the corral without hindrance.

He rolled under the rail, coming up on his feet before the scared horses could stomp him into the ground and grabbed the ears of a big skewbald. He wrestled the horse to a standstill and climbed astride. He threw his saddlebags over the animal's powerful shoulders and adjusted his holster rig so that it crossed his chest from shoulder to armpit, permitting him to slip the rifle through the temporary sling. Then he steered the horse to the nearest gate.

He kicked the poles out of the way and pointed the horse through. Behind them, the rest of the herd thundered clear, bowling Confederates before their hooves like human skittles.

Jubal didn't stop to check whether anyone else got a mount. He just gave his own its head and drummed his heels against its ribs as it charged through the camp and on out into the night. His one aim was to break free and find President Grant before Beauregard.

A sabre-wielding lieutenant of infantry, his blue-brimmed kepi askew, took a swing at Jubal as he went past. His kepi tumbled from his head as the medical bag hit him behind his right ear and he fell against the horse's withers, flying away in a sprawl of wide-flung limbs as the cavalry mount executed a neat swerve that rammed its hindquarters hard against the offending body. The two troopers accompanying the officer dived to either side as the big horse bore down on them, their carbines forgotten as they scattered.

Then Jubal saw Pickett running hard between the tents, a group of howling rebels hot on his heels.

Jubal turned the skewbald so that it charged down a canvas lined alley, hitting the foremost of the black man's pursuers at full run. Three men went down under the impact and Jubal hauled the beast around, lifting its head so that the shod hooves flailed air in the faces of the other Confederates.

One was running too hard. He raced headlong into the pounding hooves, dropping his handgun as one hoof tore away the front of his face, lifting his hands to clutch at the strips of bleeding skin that hung like fallen flags from the bloodied bones of his cheeks and forehead. Then the other hoof came down on the top of his skull, crushing it like a breakfast egg beneath the spoon. His legs stopped pumping as his nerve centre died, the linkages of tendon and muscle slackening abruptly, his legs folding under him. Jubal fought the half-crazed horse to a stop as the remaining Confederates gaped in open-mouthed horror at their dead companion. Pickett took the opportunity to grab the fallen gun and empty it into their ranks. Demoralized by the sheer audacity of the sudden reversal, the rebels ran for cover, giving Jubal the chance to lift Pickett up behind him.

'Thanks, doc.' The Negro was hanging on to Jubal as they galloped away from the blaze.

'Pleasure, sergeant,' Jubal shouted over his shoulder, 'what happened to Newman?'

'Don't rightly know,' answered Pickett, 'last I saw he was cuttin' out a pony an' tryin' to persuade Nicholls to grab one. Sailors never could ride, nohow.'

At that moment Jubal was more concerned with effecting his own escape than with the fate of Newman or the sailor's equestrian abilities. He worked the Spencer loose from its sling and passed it back to the Negro.

'Use that if you have to, but don't waste shells.'

'Doc,' came the reply, 'I been fightin' Johnny Reb since Petersburg an' Comanche after. I ain't about to waste no cartridges.'

Jubal grinned, despite the danger; he was teaching – or trying to – a professional how to fight.

'Sorry, sergeant. I didn't mean to preach to the converted.'

Then the grin was wiped off his face by a bullet. It hit his mount clean between the forequarters, travelling down the horse's body through lungs and heart before exiting between the central ribs. The horse dropped in mid-stride, catapulting both men high over its fallen head.

They were close to the camp's edge, where the tents thinned, offering little cover, and outlined by the blaze at their backs. Beauregard had put out a skirmish line of infantry to contain the breakout and Jubal and Pickett had ridden head on to the muzzles of the waiting guns. Behind him, Jubal could hear the Negro groaning; his own body hurt abominably, but pure fury was taking over, pumping adrenalin through his veins, powering his muscles to savage limits as his honed nerves screamed for action.

He was blind to the odds against him as he grabbed the Spencer and levered a shell into the breech.

Belly down on the ground, he took fast, cool aim on a flashing gun, squeezed the trigger and exulted at the scream that echoed his shot. Cold and deadly, he raked the skirmish line with fast-action fire, pumping the lever of the converted Spencer with automatic precision, his brown eyes slitted against the deceptive fire shadows as he probed the night for fresh targets. He saw men jump and twist in the macabre contortions of sudden death as he worked the rifle, and enjoyed each leaping death dance. Then the gun was empty and he stopped long enough to grab a handful of fresh cartridges from his pocket.

It was also long enough for the Confederates to regroup and mount a rush.

They came through the night screaming rebel yells as they triggered partially aimed carbines at their solitary opponent.

As they came forwards, Pickett joined Jubal, dragging the Colt, unasked, from the holster. Resting the long-barrelled gun on his left forearm, the Negro took aim as cool and deadly as Jubal's, thumbing the hammer with cold precision, dropping a charging rebel with every shot.

As he emptied the gun, Jubal was reloaded and back in the action. He rose up on one knee, working the rifle like an automated scythe designed to cut life. A solid swathe of bullets spread out across the Confederate infantry as Jubal raked their charge. Like corn in a field they fell.

And then the Spencer was empty again and the rebels still coming. Pickett unloaded six shots from the Colt before Jubal could reload the rifle, and the Confederates were on top of them.

Jubal smashed a plunging bayonet aside with the butt of the Spencer, rammed the gun into the rebel's face and rolled aside as a second blasted a shell into the ground and fell back as Jubal's feet caught him in the stomach. Then he was caught up in a rolling mess of stamping boots and stabbing blades, dodging for his life as he went down under the wave of charging men.

A blade sliced a line of red down his cheek and he drove his feet hard into the stomach of the man looming over him, hurling him back into the press of bodies. He swung the Spencer like a club, clearing a space so that he could stand up and try to stay alive. At least the length of the rifle afforded him a chance; it was long enough to deflect the probing bayonets and heavy enough to inflict damage on the attackers. Pickett was in a far worse position. Armed only with the Colt, he was taking murderous wounds from the rebel blades, blood staining the faded cloth of his blue jacket to the same dark hue as his face. Jubal began to work his way towards the Negro, parrying, clubbing, kicking as he fought through the rebels.

He felt a bayonet grate on his ribs, and wondered how long he could last as Pickett went down shouting under a rain of smashing rifle butts.

Then the charge broke as two horses hit at full gallop. Jubal saw a yelling rider jump his mount over Pickett's body, knocking rebels out of the way as it plunged headlong through the infantry. The second rider went down, his horse shot from under him, the corpse crashing a circle clear of its falling body as a rich English accent spewed curses across the night.

The first rider turned and pelted back, two handguns spitting death into the Confederate lines as the fallen man came up on his feet, using a sabre to deadly effect. Jubal recognized Newman and Nicholls and was grateful for their intervention. Somewhere back in the camp people were still fighting, a Gatling rattled a death-knell punctuated by rifle fire and the sharper *crack* of handguns. Flames lit the sky as the dry tents blazed and columns of roiling smoke spread over the dark night as fire-fighting teams fought the blaze.

Newman brought his horse to a halt as the skirmish line broke, Nicholls took a final swing at a running back, and then the rebels were gone, leaving the four escapees temporarily alone in the fiery night.

Newman threw the reins of his horse to Jubal.

'Take it and get the hell outta here.'

'What about you?' Jubal was unwilling to leave them. Newman, Pickett and Nicholls had saved his life and without horses they would have little chance of escape.

The answer came from Pickett, staggering to his feet with blood from his wounds drenching his uniform jacket.

'It's the midnight hour, doc. There ain't no place we can run to, so you take the pony an' let him run. Maybe you can reach Grant an' warn him. Try anyway.'

'Get on.' Jubal recognized the Devonshire accent of Nicholls. 'I can't ride anyway. You try and stop Beauregard.'

'That's about it, Jubal,' Newman added, 'someone has to get through, an' I figger you've got the best chance. We'll hold pursuit as long as we can. You take the horse an' find Grant.'

Jubal made a fast decision.

'O.K.' He was mounting the horse as he spoke, lashing his saddlebags and valise in place, the reloaded Spencer held in his right hand. 'Thanks.'

The three men didn't answer. They were too busy watching the line of Confederates advancing on them.

Jubal kicked the horse to a fast run through the burning tents, heading north-west to where he hoped the ambush was to take place. He hoped the three men would not die in vain, trying hard not to hear the gunfire behind him.

One by one they fell like candles in the sun. Pickett went down with a bayonet through his ribs, clubbing his murderer with the empty Colt. Nicholls cut four men to death with the sabre before a bullet shattered his skull. Newman emptied his guns into the wave of grey-clad attackers, killing three and wounding four more before a hail of bullets threw him back over Pickett's body.

They took the better part of an hour to die, giving Jubal the chance to escape.

On the ridge above the camp, Jubal paused to look back. He was too far away now to pick out individual details, but the glow of fire was bright in the dark sky. He watched for a moment, then turned the horse northwards.

'Come on,' he muttered, 'I got three debts to pay now, and one score to settle.' He thought of Beauregard and grimaced. 'Yeah. Call it the white man's burden.'

# CHAPTER THIRTEEN

He had a horse, a rifle and a set of coded maps. On his trail was a blood-hungry mob of vengeance-bent fanatics. In front of him lay a rugged wilderness. And somewhere in that wilderness the President's train was moving towards an appointment with death.

He didn't know how he was going to locate the ambush – and still less how he would stop it. But he did know he had to try.

It was one hell of a long gamble, like trying to fill a straight on one card, but there were times when the chances facing a man had to be taken and tried and all he could do was ride stone-blind into the thing and get it done. Or die doing it.

Jubal calculated that he had a good hour on his pursuers. Newman, Pickett and Nicholls had given him that long at least, so he dismounted to let the panting pony catch its breath and settled down to study the maps. His first perusal had told him little about their meanings, but now, armed with the information he had picked up in the stockade, he found he could decipher the abbreviations. The tracks of the Union Pacific from Promontory Point to Portland were marked out below the big loop of the Northern Pacific, hooking round from Butte in Montana to dive south towards the Columbia before swinging north again to Seattle.

The other, red-inked lines, had to be prospective lines, the ones Beauregard's backers wanted opened – and controlled – to make their financial killing.

That meant that the real killing, the one involving bullets and blood, would take place where the heavy red × bisected the black track of the Northern Pacific close to a town called Jamesville. Jubal turned to the Government Survey map he had bought. It was, to say the least, incomplete, but it did allow him to equate the hand-drawn maps to measured distances and locations. Jamesville lay fifty miles north-east of his present position, between Ellensburg and Seattle, lost and lonely amongst the windy ridges of the Cascades.

As he mounted he hoped the road was not too rough: it was long and lonesome enough already.

Two days later the horse put its leg into a crack and went down in a screaming flurry that pitched Jubal way out into the bristlecones lining the trail. He was swearing as he dragged himself free of the needle-sharp branches, cursing the animal and his rotten luck and Beauregard. The leg was snapped clean at the fetlock, so Jubal shot the agonized creature and began to walk. He carried the saddlebags containing his money slung over his shoulder; his medical bag was tied to his waist, leaving his hands free to use the Spencer.

He alternated his pace, running for as long as he could before slowing to a walk. He made cold camp that night, shivering without a blanket as he waited for the sun to rise. When it came up he started again. Water was available in abundance from the streams and rivulets that cut the mountains with icy precision, but he had no food, nor the time to hunt. He estimated that he had one more day to reach Jamesville; and wondered if he would make it.

He hit the ridge at noon and collapsed on to weary knees as he sighted the cluster of buildings below him. He pushed to his feet and set out in a wild run straight down the slope. Roots tripped him and naked stone bruised him as he raced headlong at the town, but he never noticed the pain, intent on reaching the sun-brightened railtracks spreading out before him.

The rail depot was about as desolate as a one-horse whistle-stop could be. Jubal dumped his gear on the timber platform and ran into the township proper. There was a low building advertising drinks and food so he pushed inside. It was empty, save for a weary-looking barman polishing glasses at one end of the table that served as bar.

'The stationman?' Jubal's voice was a lung-busted rasp. 'Where is he?'

'Tobin?' drawled the bartender, 'I can't say as I know. What you want him fer?'

'A ride,' grunted Jubal, 'right now. Where is he?'

The man scratched his balding scalp, looking quizzically at the tattered, dirty figure staring at him.

'Like I said, I don't rightly know.'

He broke off as Jubal lifted the Spencer, working the lever so that the cocked rifle pointed at his chest.

'You got exactly three seconds to tell me,' rasped Jubal. 'After that I'll kill you and find someone else to ask.'

'Waal,' the barkeep scratched his head again, 'I ain't too sure ...'

He broke off as a bullet lifted tufts of hair from what was left of his scanty brown locks. Jubal crossed the room in three steps and rammed the Spencer hard into his stomach. As the man doubled up, he clipped the muzzle against his chin, snapped the lever and shoved the barrel against the barkeep's cheek.

'You want to lose your head,' Jubal said coldly, 'you keep it up and see what happens.'

The man was weeping with fear, mumbling through his bruised lips, but he managed to get out the information Jubal wanted.

Five minutes later, Tobin, protesting at the interruption of his lunch, was marching hurriedly down the street, prodded on by Jubal's gun. He was trying to explain that no trains were due through until the Presidential Special the next morning.

Jubal ignored him: he wanted transport and planned to get it. Any way he could. He ate the remains of Tobin's lunch as he went; he was too hungry to worry overmuch about the source, and if one recalcitrant railwayman went hungry for a while, it was small recompense for a little place in the history books. Providing, of course, that anyone ever heard about the episode.

He prodded Tobin up on to the low platform, deaf to the man's protests as he demanded the whereabouts of the depot's handcart.

Mouthing his protests all the way, Tobin opened a shed and hauled out the hand-cranked vehicle. Jubal was helping him manhandle the cart on to the rails when a familiar voice interrupted his efforts.

'Howdy, friend Jubal. You're sure lookin' a mite worse fer the wear.'

Jubal didn't bother reaching for the Spencer: he knew Ahab's buffalo gun would be levelled at him and the big black dog poised to spring.

'Hallo, Ahab.' He turned around as he spoke, ignoring Tobin who was gaping at the one-legged man and his canine partner. 'You got one hell of a habit of cropping up where you're not expected.'

'Keeps me alive, son,' Ahab chuckled. He gestured at the handcart. 'Takes two to trolley them things. You need a hand?'

'Heading for Jamesville,' grunted Jubal as he pushed the wheels into place on the rails, 'you want to lend a hand, you're welcome.'

'Good.' Ahab's cackle was sinister with hidden intent, his pale blue eyes sparkling like cold fire. 'Figger there'll be a man I want to meet there.'

He motioned Strife on to the small platform that was all the passenger space on the cart and climbed aboard himself, setting his rifle beside him. Jubal was surprised, but Ahab was a surprising kind of man, so he slung his own gun on to the cart and manned one end of the long, see-saw handle that worked the drive mechanism of the trolley. Ahab grabbed the other T-bar and began to pump.

It was back-breaking, lung-busting work to drive the cart up the gradient leading out of town, but they made it to the first rise and then watched the brake as they careened down the far slope with Strife snarling anxiously at the unaccustomed wind-rush of their passage. Jubal took the opportunity to question Ahab; the old man had cropped up too often since their first meeting way back south of Albuquerque. Whatever his mission, it seemed pretty clear that it was tied in with Jubal's own desperate journey.

Ahab grinned, showing his blackened teeth, and reached down to ruffle Strife's rising hackles.

'Ain't you figgered it out yet?' His grin stretched his leath-

129

ery face taut, so it looked even more like the face of some dried-out corpse. 'I'm lookin' fer Beauregard. Mordecai Beauregard.' His smile turned into a snarl that brought the dog halfway to its feet. 'A man with a soul as black as his skin's white.'

He paused as they cranked the trolley along a flat stretch of track.

'He owes me three things. Four, if you count in his life. I got me a nice little spread back in 59. Down in Dansas, it was; little timber two-roomer I built myself, an' a parcel o' land to go with it. Figgered to raise cows. Figgered to bring my woman out from Georgia.'

Jubal watched the oldster's face as he spoke. As near as he could guess, Ahab was looking sad.

'I brung her out in 61. Two months afore the war got started. Good months, they were. Before I joined up. Rode north an' signed with the Union. Went through Antietam an' Gettysburg, then I got shot in 64.

'I went back home on sick leave an' two days after I arrived we got hit by a bunch o' Kansas raiders. Took a slug in my knee an' lay in that bloody Kansas dirt yellin' while my place burned down.' The cold blue eyes turned to pure ice, burning into Jubal's as the old man spoke the next sentences. 'I watched the Rebs rape my wife an' I watched them shoot her down like a dog when they was finished. I couldn't stand up to bury her, so I crawled nine miles afore I got picked up by a neighbour. I woke up in a Union hospital with my leg gone.

'I woke up rememberin' the man who headed the raiders. He's kinda hard to forget, bein' bleach-bone white with eyes as red as hellfire. I remember him laughin' while they raped my wife.

'I been lookin' fer him ever since. Army didn't want me no more, so I had the time.'

He spat over the edge of the handcart.

'Kinda funny when you think about it. Ole Beauregard was supposed to be guerrilla raidin' then. It musta taken a whole chunk o' fightin' time to hit one no-account spread in Kansas.

'So there're the things he owes me: my woman, my leg an'

130

my spread. An' his life.'

He grabbed the handcart's lever and pumped as though trying to exorcize a personal demon. Jubal matched his vigour for his own reasons, he had his own credit list of death and destruction tallied up against Beauregard's account. But one thing about Ahab still bothered him.

'How come you keep turning up on my trail?' he shouted between swings of the trolley's lever.

'Hell, ain't it obvious?' Ahab grinned. 'I was trailin' Tyree, figgered the wagon train would lead me to ole Beau'. When he gave you that package I thought you was one o' them. Then I decided to trail you an' find out if I was right. I thought about killin' you, but I needed a lead to the hideout, so I jest got rid o' Canfield an' Sillers to hurry you along a bit.

'When I saw you bein' whipped I reckoned I was wrong about you. Me an' Strife was comin' in to rescue you, only you broke out first. So damn' thoroughly I couldn't even spot ole Beau' in the confusion: his camp's real burned out now.

'Knowin' him, though, he ain't about to let you get away free, so I picked up yore trail an' found you again. Ole Beau' will be headin' in yore direction. Only I'll be waitin' fer him.'

'I guess,' grinned Jubal, 'that we both got scores to settle. Between us, we should bleed the albino white.'

# CHAPTER FOURTEEN

Sparks screeched from the protesting metal of the wheels as they braked the handcart to a stop in the centre of Jamesville. The lines bisected the town, running dead centre down the length of the widest street, with lines of brightly coloured bunting decorating the stores and saloons. Ropes traversed the street, carrying Old Glory and a succession of hand-painted canvas sheets welcoming the President to Jamesville. The whole place was set up for a full-scale carnival.

So Jubal wondered why it was so quiet.

He found out when the swing doors of the nearest saloon flew open to expose a grey uniform. The man wore a sabre on his left hip and an empty holster on his right. The pistol was in his hand, pointing at Jubal. Beneath the brim of his grey cavalry stetson he was grinning like a wolverine closing for the kill.

'Welcome to Jamesville, gentlemen. Leave your weapons where they are and walk slowly over here.'

Jubal grabbed the Spencer and powered himself off the handcart. He hit the road shoulder first, levering a shell into the breech as he rolled to his feet. Beside him, Ahab leaped to the ground followed by the dog as grey uniforms appeared all along the street. Gunfire broke the false tranquillity of Jamesville as the fugitives raced for cover. They were exposed, but had the advantage of being between two lines of rebels, so that the Confederate fire threatened to hit friends as much as foes. Jubal saw the chance and headed fast for a sidestreet.

He reached the entrance and ran on far enough to get out of sight of his pursuers. Then he dropped to all fours and crawled under the raised boardwalk.

The space was dark and dirty, thick with dust and crawling insects. Jubal ignored them and burrowed in amongst the litter, dragging himself forwards until he reached the far side

132

of the building. Panting, he lay face down, listening to the shouting behind him, hoping that Beauregard's men would forget to look under the building.

He heard boots pound across the planks over his head and a shouted curse followed by Strife's deep-throated bark. Man and dog both fell abruptly quiet; footsteps echoed over Jubal, a door banged and he heard orders shouted. His two companions were under guard in a room above him. He decided that they could stay there while he checked out the town. Silent as a stalking cat, he worked his way back from mainstreet to the corner of the boardwalk, where it ran around the edge of the block. Cautiously, he edged out, Spencer cocked and ready to fire, but no target showed so he darted to the shelter of the far building.

Jamesville was not a large town so Jubal made the outskirts quickly, emerging where a wide, tree-covered slope banked down to the edge of town. He slipped in amongst the trees and began to climb.

Ten minutes later he stopped and hauled himself up through the branches of a big pine. He was several hundred feet above Jamesville now and able to spot most of Beauregard's positions. Two of the 32-pounder cannons were located at the farther end of mainstreet, one aimed straight down the rail tracks so that its ball would hit any oncoming engine head on, the second at an angle off to one side, where it could command town and rail line alike. A squadron of cavalry was checking equipment in a stockyard three blocks back from the central thoroughfare, and numerous rooftops sported grey-uniformed men clutching long-barrelled sniper's rifles.

The odds were formidable, and as Jubal shinned down the tree he decided that he could use an ally.

Then he halted his descent, staring away to the west. Faintly through the pines and ridges of the Cascades he could see a plume of black smoke drifting across the sky. He followed it down towards the ground, and saw that its source was moving, seemingly slowly at that distance, towards Jamesville. He was too far away to spot details, but he knew the smoke could have only one source: Grant's train.

133

He hit the ground in a rush and hurled himself down the slope into Jamesville.

Back in the town he was forced to exercise caution in his movements, slipping from the protection of one building to another as he worked his way to Ahab's prison. He spotted the place without anyone seeing him, a small hotel with only one entrance, guarded by a young trooper carrying a single-shot Henry.

Jubal moved like a wraith through the silent town, closing on the trooper. He reached the block containing the hotel and paused, then he climbed the porch rail and pushed his rifle up on to the veranda roof, pulling himself up after. On hands and knees, he clambered along the shingles until he was directly above the guard. He perched on the very edge of the flimsy roof and reached a cartridge from his pocket, then he threw it hard at the farther boardwalk.

Bobby Vincent had been daydreaming of his folks' farm back in Tennessee, wondering how the hogs were doing nowadays. He was thirsty as all hell, wishing he could take a good, big swig of his pappy's moonshine.

He died thinking about it. When the cartridge bounced off the planks he was only halfway alert as he stepped across to investigate the sudden noise. Jubal came off the roof feet first, his boots slamming into Bobby's back, crushing ribs and pitching the young rebel flat on his face. Before he could lift his mouth out of the dust to yell, Jubal brought the butt of the Spencer down as hard as he could on the back of Bobby's head.

The fragile bone crumbled like an eggshell, and for a moment Bobby tasted the moonshine he was dreaming about. Then the world went out as Bobby Vincent died.

Jubal twisted and crossed the boardwalk in three long strides. He went in through the door like a human battering-ram, hurling the guard inside straight across the room. As the man stumbled, Ahab lifted out of a chair, bringing his pegleg up to drive into the soldier's stomach. The man doubled up, letting his carbine fall as he clutched at his belly. Ahab fell on to him, scrawny fingers seeking his windpipe, closing and squeezing as the man's eyes bulged with the effort of sucking air into empty lungs.

A third trooper did his best to cock his rifle before Jubal swung the Spencer like a club, laying the metal of the barrel across his temple. The rebel fell as though shot, his gun still uncocked.

Jubal turned as Ahab finished off the other man and reached for his huge Sharps. He checked the breech as Jubal explained the situation, then limped to a side door where snarls reverberated through the woodwork. With the big black dog at his side, hackles standing stiff with anticipation, he studied Jubal through cold blue eyes.

'Like I told you, Jubal.' His voice was cold as a graveyard in winter. 'I come here fer ole Beau'. Now if that means I gotta help you save the President, I'll do it. But Beauregard's my target.'

Jubal accepted the compromise, leading the way out of the hotel with Ahab and Strife close on his heels.

They hugged the back alleys and yards as they worked their way through Jamesville towards the cannons. Twice they ran into patrolling rebels and twice the Confederates died silently, caught by surprise before they could raise the alarm. Then the element of surprise was lost to them: the first cannon was set squarely in the centre of the street, dragged out since Jubal had first spotted it to allow a completely clear field of fire. Squads of infantry flanked the gun, denying them the chance of even a sudden rush.

'Looks like Grant's about to get a nasty shock,' muttered Ahab, 'there ain't no way we're gonna reach that thing alive.'

'There has to be a way,' snarled Jubal, watching the approaching column of smoke, 'let's check the other cannon.'

They pulled back from the water butts that sheltered them and ran through the deserted streets to the second gun emplacement. The Confederates were grouping on mainstreet, gathering around doorways and carefully placed wagons, weapons kept mostly out of sight as they awaited the train. Jubal could hear the whistle now, blasting shrilly through the mountain air as the engine-driver did his best to warn Jamesville of the President's approach.

On the rooftops, the snipers edged into position; the cavalry walked their horses from the stockpens, standing ready in the sidestreets for a flanking charge. Standing tall and white on the platform erected for Grant's ceremonial speech stood Beauregard, dressed in the full ceremonial uniform of a Confederate General. Ahab saw him and swore violently, wiping a bead of spittle on to the foresight of the buffalo gun. He dropped to one knee and sighted the big gun, then a group of officers joined the commander, shutting him off from view. Ahab cursed again.

'Damn it,' Jubal snarled, 'let's find that cannon first. After that you can go hunting your private game.'

'Like I tole you, Jubal,' grunted the old man, 'it's ole Beau' I want. He's the bird I'm after.'

'So kill two with one stone,' grated Jubal, listening to the nearing whistle, 'but let's stop that cannon first.'

Reluctantly, Ahab climbed to his feet and followed Jubal down the alley. Two blocks on they hit the second cannon. It was situated in a square formed by the angle of two streets around the empty plot of an unbuilt building. Sheltered from view of the main drag, it was angled to lob shells over the building on the nearest corner down on to the street beyond. The square was cut off on three sides by the surrounding houses, the fourth opening on to mainstreet. Beauregard had obviously felt the position safe, because only six troopers stood guard around the 32-pounder, standing tense as the gunners primed the piece. One man dropped a charge down the bore as a second stood ready with the rammer, the other four artillerymen fussing around the sights.

'Twelve to two,' whispered Ahab, 'you fancy the odds, Jubal?'

'Twelve to three,' Jubal replied, 'we got the dog, as well.'

Ahab grinned and cocked the buffalo gun.

'O.K., you call it.'

Jubal called it with a shot that dropped one of the infantrymen in his tracks. Then he levered the action of the Spencer with deadly precision, raking the Confederates with murder-

136

ously accurate fire. Beside him, Ahab's Sharps bellowed three times, then he was on his feet, running at the gun. Four guards and three gunners were dead, the fifth infantryman levelled a bayonet at Jubal and met his charge. Then Strife flew through the air ahead of Jubal, bowling the rebel over as long yellow fangs sank deep into his throat. The man died trying to push the monster dog away from him; it was a futile attempt, that ended when Strife fell back with most of the trooper's throat clutched in his dripping jaws.

Four artillerymen remained, gaping at the trio confronting them. Jubal made a fast decision.

'Fire it!' He barked the words as he pushed fresh shells into the Spencer.

The gunnery captain objected. Jubal levered the Spencer and shot the rebel in the stomach.

The officer screamed and fell back on to the cannon, frothy red blood decorating his blond moustache as he clutched at the hole in his belly. Jubal kicked him off the gun and levelled the rifle at the others.

'Fire it,' he snarled again. 'Unless you want the same treatment.'

The first blast lifted high over the buildings flanking mainstreet. It was an incendiary shell that exploded close to Beauregard's platform. The Confederates scattered for cover as the splashing flame took hold on the woodwork, confusion spreading with the dancing fire. The second shell spread a curtain of flame across the street, taking hold on the wooden frontages of Jamesville. Through the roar of the spreading fire, Jubal could hear the shrilling whistle of the train, too close now to stop outside the town, and the shouts of the Confederate rebels as they sought their attackers.

'Guess we better move out,' he barked.

'Yeah,' agreed Ahab, 'but first . . .'

He had picked up a fallen Colt which he used on the gunners, shooting the three terrified men where they stood. Then he joined Jubal in a one-legged run for mainstreet.

The flames were spreading, dancing along the lines of bunting, blistering tarpaper roofs and taking hold on dry timber fronts as Beauregard tried to bring his command to order. At the far end of the burning town, Jubal could see the presidential train blowing steam as the engineer fought it to a sliding, screaming halt. Then he spotted Beauregard running for the other cannon. He saw a sabre lift high and drop, the big gun kick back against its stabilizing ropes, the puff of smoke from the muzzle.

The shot hit the train square in the boiler, smashing it back against the tender. Like some wounded monster, the engine lifted up and over, slowly, steam pouring from the ruptured frontplate. Then it fell on its side and exploded as the carriages ploughed into the wreckage.

Beauregard lost half the men running for the train in the explosion. They plunged headlong into the blast of erupting boilers, falling to the screaming shards of broken metal that filled the street like shrapnel, pressing blistered hands to boiled eyeballs as the steam hit them. More fell to the gunfire that blasted from the two standing carriages as blue-clad soldiers poured out on to the smoky roadway, and still more to the fire that Jubal put down.

Ahab disappeared into the roiling smoke, hunting his own prey with the big black dog pacing at his side. Jubal let him go as he ran headlong into the fires.

He saw a heavily built man with a plain blue uniform stumbling from a wrecked coach and moved to help him. As he hauled the bearded man to his feet from the dust where he had fallen, he caught the odour of whiskey on the man's breath. He was swearing volubly, fumbling inside his tunic as though looking for a wound. Jubal was about to lay him down when the big, rough hand emerged wrapped around a silver flask. With a sigh of relief, the black-haired man took a long swallow and pushed the flask at Jubal.

'Thanks, son.' His voice was slurred with drink. 'You want a shot?'

'No.' Jubal was losing his temper. 'I want the President. Grant.'

'You got him.' The bearded man slapped Jubal heartily on the back. 'I'm Grant. President of the United States of

America. Though they ain't too united up here to judge from those Johnny Reb grey-coats I been seeing. Who the hell are you?'

'Jubal Cade.' He wasn't used to half-drunk presidents. 'You rode into an ambush.'

Grant bellowed laughter across the burning street.

'Dammit, boy, I seen more ambushes than you've eaten breakfasts. You think that fuckin' war was some kind of picnic? Now you go find me a gun an' I'll pitch in to clear up a few more Confederate whoresons.'

Jubal grabbed a pistol from a corpse in the street, thought again, and took the cartridge belt. He handed them to Ulysses S. Grant, and watched the President amble off into the smoke, shouting orders at the gold-braided officers clustering around him.

Then he heard the familiar thunder of Strife's bark and headed for the sound.

Jamesville was a sea of flame and fighting men. The Confederate cavalry had swung out as the train crashed, to be met by the concentrated fire of Grant's guard. Confined within the roadway, the rebels were falling back in confusion, their horses shying at the flames created by Jubal and Ahab. The infantry, with central command and one cannon gone, were milling in confusion, falling in sporadic struggles against the Union troops and the angry townsfolk.

Jubal pushed through the fighting, looking for Ahab and the dog and Beauregard.

He found them together, suddenly, as the smoke of the burning town cleared for a moment. He saw Strife launch his huge black body at Beauregard, jaws stretched wide to expose the yellow, slavering teeth, ready for the deadly throat lunge. Then the sabre in the albino's hand thrust forwards, lifting up, held firm on a stiffened arm to meet the dog's leap.

Beauregard fell to one knee as the dog sprang at him. It was a hideously perfect manoeuvre that spitted the dog clean through the chest. Jubal saw the point of the sword enter Strife's chest, the dripping red blade emerging from between the dog's shoulder-blades. Strife was dead as soon as the sabre punctured him, but his jaws were still reaching for Beauregard's throat as his weight dragged the sword from the albino's hand, and he kept on snarling until the blood clogged his throat and he whined and barked and died.

The white-skinned rebel sprang to his feet, reaching for the gun on his right hip as Ahab rose up like some single-legged spectre of revenge.

The ·50 calibre Sharps was pointed at Beauregard's chest, hammer thumbed back as a smile like a death-knell spread across Ahab's withered features.

'Been a long time, Beau'.' His voice was flat and dead and cold. 'An' I guess it's the last time.'

'Don't do it, Ahab.' Beauregard was pulling the Colt Dragoon as he spoke. 'You can't kill kin.'

'Like hell I can't,' snarled Ahab as he squeezed the trigger.

The Sharps thundered through the smoke. Beauregard was no more than four feet from the muzzle, so the heavy bullet lifted him high off his feet, hurling him yards back as a great, gaping red hole blossomed on his grey tunic. He hit the boardwalk and bounced once, decorating the planking with a huge red smear. Incredibly, he tried to lift up to his feet, grabbing for the rail, and pulling halfway to his feet before Ahab's second bullet hit his face.

The ·50 calibre ball took him between his pink eyes, mashing the centre of his face to the same colour as his skull shattered under the impact. Crimson-stained brain matter splattered over his grey uniform as he pitched backwards, his white hair darkening as the blood spread in a wide pool from the emptied gap of his cranium. Jubal looked down into a big hole where Beauregard's eyes had once been and then up to Ahab.

For the first time, the old man looked to be at peace.

'Hell of a thing, ain't it?' he asked. 'Two men want the same woman. One gets her, an' the other can't forgive them. So he don't stop at nothin' to spoil it fer them. It was like that with me an' Beau'.'

He stooped to lift the shattered body of the Confederate in his arms.

'Guess I should bury him now. After all, he was my brother.'

Jubal watched the one-legged man walk away through the smoke, following his lean body until he was gone from sight with his bloody burden, then he turned back to the town.

The fighting was mostly finished, Grant's troops mopping up the demoralized rebels. It was, he thought, as he paced back through the fires consuming Jamesville, typical of the Frontier to erupt into mindless violence; it had been that way when he left America, that way ever since he came back. He was a doctor, yet every step he took seemed to lead to more killing. He walked slowly back to the handcart; his medical valise and the saddlebags were still there, so he picked them up and headed towards the nearest stable. He wanted a horse to take him back to St. Louis.

A gruff voice interrupted his thoughts.

'Been hearin' about how it was you stopped this attack.' Grant offered his flask as he spoke, and Jubal accepted it this time. 'So why not stick around an' take a ride back east?'

Jubal swallowed and nodded his agreement.

'Yeah, why not?' he murmured. 'I don't have too many other places to go.'